D1055096

IPL Library of Crime Classics®
presents
**THE COMPLEAT
ADVENTURES OF DR. SAM:
JOHNSON, DETECTOR**

✛

DR. SAM: JOHNSON, DETECTOR

✛

**THE DETECTIONS OF DR. SAM:
JOHNSON**

✛

**THE RETURN OF DR. SAM:
JOHNSON, DETECTOR**

✛

**THE EXPLOITS OF DR. SAM:
JOHNSON, DETECTOR***

*forthcoming

THE RETURN
of DR. SAM: JOHNSON, DETECTOR

as told *by* JAMES BOSWELL

"I am lost without my Boswell."
Sherlock Holmes

by
Lillian de la Torre

New York: imprinted for INTERNATIONAL
POLYGONICS, LIMITED, Booksellers, at the sign of
the *Polygon*, to be had wherever Books are sold.

1985

THE RETURN OF DR. SAM: JOHNSON, DETECTOR

Stories: Copyright © 1947, 1972, 1974, 1978 by
Lillian de la Torre.
Copyright renewed 1975 by Lillian de la Torre.
Introduction and new material. Copyright © 1985 by
Lillian de la Torre.
Cover and artwork: Copyright © 1985 by International
Polygonics, Ltd.
With the exception of ''The Disappearing Servant
Wench'', the contents of this volume first appeared in
Ellery Queen's Mystery Magazine.
Book design by Jennifer Place
Library of Congress Catalog No. 85-81383
ISBN 0-930330-34-X
Printed and manufactured in the United States of
America

First book publication November 1985
10 9 8 7 6 5 4 3 2 1

DEDICATION

To my beloved Theodore and Evelyn,
who share the ''Johnsonian aether.''

FOREWORD

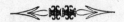

Once upon a time I had an argument with my husband, the Professor. I usually forget an argument as soon as it is over, but I have never forgotten this one, for its consequences were far-reaching.

The Professor was decrying my favorite reading, detective stories.

"Detectives, bosh!" he snorted. "Drawling dilettantes, cute brides, sententious Chinamen, dear old ladies—next thing, I suppose, a police dog!"

"There's been a police dog," I admitted. "Granted, if the detective's flimsy, the story's flimsy. But if the detective is a solid and many-sided personality, like—like, for instance, Dr. Sam: Johnson in Boswell's great biography—"

As the words left my lips, I knew what I had. Here was a real man as versatile and various as any fictitious detective, just and humane, with wide-ranging interests and flavorful personality; a man of undaunted valor, keen intellect, and scientific curiosity. What a detective he would make! And he came equipped with his Boswell, the only original Boswell, a fascinating character in his own right, with his amatory exploits, his flair for sensation, and his gift of observation.

And the two friends flourished in the English Age of Reason, the 18th Century, a time of awakening scientific curiosity and humanitarian regard for the fate of the individual. As Howard Haycraft has pointed out, detective interest could hardly have come along sooner. In earlier days, "whodunit" was not the point. If a Montague was murdered, the thing to do was not to ask questions, but to go out and poignard a Capulet. Any Capulet would do.

The urge to ask questions, the appetite for facts, may be dated, in England, from the founding of the Royal Society in 1660. Then experimental science began to flourish, and gradually that inquiring habit of mind began to be brought to bear on the investigation of crime.

It was in 1698 that the first expert witnesses appeared in court to narrate experiments they had performed which proved the innocence of the accused, a lawyer named Spencer Cowper. In 1733, faced with a locked-room murder, the authorities demonstrated the classic string trick in open court. (See "Murder Lock'd In".) In 1770, footsteps in the snow were first fitted to the shoes that made them. In 1783 the ingenious Captain Donellan was detected distilling and administering the first fatal dose of prussic acid, and was duly hanged for it.

These were only beginnings. There was as yet no such thing as a *detective*. Scotland Yard only came into being in the next century. Before that, the law was represented on the one hand by the watch, ineffective old "Charlies" hired by each parish to cry the hours and keep the peace if they could; and on the other hand by professional thief-takers like Jonathan Wild, who would cheerfully swear away your life for money; while trading Justices in Bow Street plundered your pockets in the middle.

As the 18th century advanced, Bow Street began to know honest magistrates like Henry Fielding, the novelist. Later his brother Sir John Fielding flourished, the famous "Blind Beak of Bow Street," with his sturdy second in command, Saunders Welch. These latter were Dr. Johnson's friends, and from them he learned about crime. "Johnson, who had an eager and unceasing curiosity to know human life in all its variety, told me," records Boswell, "that he attended Mr. Welch in his office for a whole winter, to hear the examinations of the culprits."

Here in a word is the answer to a question that high-minded people often ask. Why is crime so fascinating? Because there is no better way to learn about human life in all its variety. It reveals man under stress, wound up to his highest pitch. A crime, so to speak, blows off the roof of man's privacy, and the law, the press, and public curiosity focus a great spotlight on everyone involved, innocent or guilty. In the ensuing investigation, in the trial which follows, everyone stands pitilessly revealed, victim, bystanders and culprit alike, all caught in the spotlight glare.

The 18th-century criminal enjoyed his full share of the spotlight. Vast mobs crowded to Tyburn Hill to see him hanged. There on the spot they could, and many did, purchase for sixpence his "Last Dying Speech and Confession" (whether or not he had made one), ghosted by some Grub Street hack. Those who missed the show could still gloat over the malefactor's misdeeds in doggerel broadside ballads, or collections of "Newgate Lives," or even a full-scale folio transcript of some notorious trial, all of which poured from the presses throughout the century, turning an honest penny for the printers and keeping crime in the spotlight.

The 18th century was rich in picturesque culprits to take the spotlight, highwaymen and footpads, frauds and forgers. Dr. Sam: Johnson interested himself in the forgers and the frauds. He even wrote the last dying speech and confession of one of them, Dr. Dodd, the fashionable "macaroni parson," who had augmented his emoluments with some quiet sleight-of-pen work, and was hanged for it. Visiting Bristol, he studied the literary forgeries of Thomas Chatterton, the "marvellous boy," and pronounced him, correctly, both a fraud and a genius. When "Ossian" Macpherson produced "an ancient epic poem translated from the Gaelic," Dr. Johnson immediately perceived it to be a contemporary fake, and denounced it as such. "Do you think," demanded a believer, "that any man of modern age could have written such poems?" "Yes, sir," replied Johnson contemptuously, "many men, many women, and many children!" Naturally Macpherson, a surly Scot, waxed irate. When he sent Johnson a threatening letter, the sage replied truculently, "I will not be deterred from detecting what I think a cheat by the menaces of a ruffian." (Note the word "detecting." He knew what he was doing.) It was for defence against Macpherson's threats that he purchased his famous oaken stick.

His curiosity about the world ranged wide. He gratified it by performing chemical experiments in Thrale's garden shed, with such enthusiasm that Mrs. Thrale feared he would blow them all up. He was open-minded enough to seek evidence of the supernatural world; but when he probed the matter of the Cock Lane Ghost and wrote up the results, he was forced to conclude that Scratching Fanny was no ghost at all. "He expressed great indignation at the imposture of the Cock Lane Ghost," says Boswell, "and related, with much satisfaction, how he had assisted in detecting the cheat." (Detecting again!)

James Boswell, Dr. Johnson's disciple and biographer, was by profession a lawyer. He too was fascinated by the world of mystery and crime, but his point of view was more sensational. His approach to a forger—the intriguing lady forger, Mrs. Rudd—was to make love to her and take her along to ride the circuit with him. He haunted executions with "horrid eagerness," and badgered condemned men to reveal their tremors. He was avid for such sensational experiences, and wrote them all up, in his letters, in his diaries, and in the newspapers.

The late Colonel Ralph Isham, who restored the Boswell Papers to the world, in general seemed to regard my inventions with indulgence. He did protest to me, however, that in them I was making Boswell appear too much of a poltroon. This I firmly denied, pointing out that Boswell liked to savor and record *all* his emotions, including fear. At Inchkenneth, for instance, he visited the ruined chapel by night, was gratified to experience "a pleasing awful confusion," and came back in haste, as Dr. Johnson told Mrs. Thrale, "for fear of spectres." Again, calling on Mrs. Rudd, he alarmed himself pleasurably with apprehensions of both bullies lurking in the kitchen and ghosts haunting the parlor. Neither thought kept him from amorous dalliance. When in Scotland he lost a client to the gallows, the very sight of the victim in his grave clothes struck him, he records, "with a kind of tremor." Tremors, however, did not prevent him from plotting boldly (though abortively) to resuscitate the still-warm cadaver when the hangman was through with it.

Like Sherlock Holmes and Dr. Watson a century later, Johnson and Boswell perambulated the most facinating of cities, London. "He who is tired of London," observed Dr. Johnson, "is tired of life." Theirs, however, was a London with a difference—not the fog-bound metropolis that Conan Doyle etched, but the sparkling city that Canaletto painted.

There they found a chiaroscuro of contrasts, from high elegance to the lowest of wretchedness. The macaronis of the Dilettanti Club donned taffeta caftans of Roman purple to toast the arts of antiquity. The rakes of the Hell-Fire Club assumed monkish garb and conjured up the Devil. Balloonists in gaudy "aerostatic globes" rose in air.

Meanwhile in nighted churchyards bodysnatchers dug up dead men for anatomists to dissect. Abandoned children slept in doorways. (Dr. Johnson, passing by, liked to surprise such waifs, now and then, with a sixpence slipped into the sleeping hand.)

Inhumanity was rife. The lunatics in Bedlam were treated as a kind of impromptu Grand Guignol show. Superannuated black slaves, turned out to beg or starve in the streets, were curses with heartless jocosity as "St. Giles Blackbirds;" while able-bodied fugitives were transported in chains to the horrors of Jamaica. Slavery in every aspect incensed the humane Dr. Johnson, who thought that all men were by nature free (though he was sometimes not so sure about Americans).

Such were the men, and such was the setting, that flashed into my mind that day. Soon plots of mystery and detection began to form theselves around many of the striking events, the picturesque scenes, and the eccentric personalities of that fascinating time; and Dr. Sam: Johnson as *detector* dominated them all.

To the best of my knowledge, I was the first—but not the last—to weave such stories around a real historical character for a detective. I was certainly the first to select a historical character who already had his Boswell to narrate his adventures.

Writing as James Boswell, I found it a challenge to use the rhetoric and vocabulary that he would have used, and no other. He made a point of adhering to certain old-style spellings, and so do I. Dr. Johnson's words come sometimes from the record, sometimes from my imagination as I conceive he would have spoken.

Boswell said of himself that he had become "impregnated with the Johnsonian aether." I should like to think that the "Johnsonian aether" permeates my tales, and that in fictitiously presenting Dr. Sam: Johnson as a *detector* of crime and chicane, righting wrongs and penetrating mysteries, I have made him act in a manner that is always consistent with the real man as he walked the earth two hundred years ago.

Lillian de la Torre

TABLE OF CONTENTS

Murder Lock'd In, *page 17*

The Bedlam Bam, *page 41*

The Disappearing Servant Wench, *page 67*

The Blackamoor Unchain'd, *page 93*

The Lost Heir, *page 115*

The Resurrection Men, *page 143*

Milady Bigamy, *page 163*

MURDER LOCK'D IN

"Murder! Murder lock'd in!"

With these horrifying words began my first experience of the *detective* genius of the great Dr. Sam: Johnson, him who—but let us proceed in order.

The '63 was to me a memorable year; for in it I had the happiness to obtain the acquaintance of that extraordinary man. Though then but a raw Scotch lad of two-and-twenty, I had already read the WORKS OF JOHNSON with delight and instruction, and imbibed therefrom the highest reverence for their authour. Coming up to London in that year, I came with the firm resolution to win my way into his friendship.

On Monday, the 16th of May, I was sitting in the back-parlour of Tom Davies, book-seller and some-time actor, when the man I sought to meet came unexpectedly into the shop. Glimpsing him through the glass-door, Davies in sepulchral tone announced his approach as of Hamlet's ghost: "Look, my Lord, it comes!"

I scrambled to my feet as the great man entered,

his tall, burly form clad in mulberry stuff of full-skirted antique cut, a large bushy greyish wig surmounting his strong-cut features of classical mould.

"I present Mr. Boswell—" began Davies. If he intended to add "from Scotland," I cut him off.

"Don't tell him where I come from!" I cried, having heard of the great man's prejudice against Scots.

"From Scotland!" cried Davies roguishly.

"Mr. Johnson," said I—for not yet had he become "Doctor" Johnson, though as such I shall always think of him—"Mr. Johnson, I do indeed come from Scotland, but I cannot help it."

"That, sir, I find," quipped Johnson with a smile, "is what a great many of your countrymen cannot help!"

This jest, I knew, was aimed at the hordes of place-seekers who "could not help coming from" Scotland to seek their fortunes in London when Scottish Lord Bute became first minister to the new King; but it put me out of countenance.

"Don't be uneasy," Davies whispered me at parting, "I can see he likes you very well!"

Thus encouraged, I made bold to wait upon the philosopher the very next Sunday, in his chambers in the Temple, where the benchers of the law hold sway. I strode along Fleet Street, clad in my best; my new bloom-coloured coat, so I flattered myself, setting off my neat form and dark, sharp-cut features. As I walked along, I savoured in anticipation this, my first encounter with the lion in his den, surrounded by his learned volumes and the tools of his trade.

But it was not yet to be, for as I turned under the arch into Inner Temple Lane, I encountered the philosopher issuing from his doorway in full Sunday panoply. His mulberry coat was well brushed, his wig was new-powdered, he wore a clean linen neckcloth and fresh bands to his wrists.

"Welcome, Mr. Boswell," said he cordially, "you are welcome to the Temple. As you see, I am just now going forth. Will you not walk along with me? I go to wait on Mistress Lennon the poetess, who dwells here in the Temple, but a step across the gardens, in Bayfield Court. Come, I will present you at her levee."

"With all my heart, sir," said I, pleased to go among the wits, and in such company.

But as it turned out, I never did present myself at the literary levee, for as we came to Bayfield Court, a knot of people buzzing about the door caught us up in their concerns.

"Well met, Mr. Johnson," called a voice, "we have need of your counsel. We have sent for the watch, but he does not come, the sluggard."

"The watch? What's amiss, ma'am?"

A babble of voices answered him. Every char-woman known to Bayfield Court, it seemed, seethed in a swarm before the entry.

"Old Mrs. Duncom—locked in, and hears no knock—here's Mrs. Taffety come to dine—"

A dozen hands pushed forward an agitated lady in a capuchin.

"Invited, Mr. Johnson, two o'clock the hour, and Mrs. Duncom don't answer. I fear the old maid is ill and the young maid is gone to fetch the surgeon, and Mrs. Duncom you know has not the use of her limbs."

"We must rouze her. Come, Mrs. Taffety, I'll make myself heard, I warrant."

The whole feminine contingent, abandoning hope of the watch, escorted us up the stair. As we mounted, I took stock of our posse. The benchers of the law, their employers, were off on their Sunday occasions, but the servitors were present in force. I saw an Irish wench with red hair and a turned-up nose, flanked close by a couple of lanky, ill-conditioned lads, probably sculls to the benchers and certainly admirers to the wench. A dark wiry little gypsy of a woman with alert black eyes boosted along a sturdy motherly soul addressed by all as Aunt Moll. Sukey and Win and Juggy, twittering to each other, followed after.

Arrived at the attick landing, Dr. Johnson raised his voice and called upon Mrs. Duncom in rolling stentorian tones. Mrs. Taffety seconded him, invoking the maids in a thin screech: "Betty! Annet!" Dead silence answered them.

"Then we must break in the door." said Dr. Johnson.

Indeed he looked abundantly capable of effecting such a feat single-handed; but at that moment a stumble of feet upon the stair proclaimed the arrival of the watch. "Hold!" cried that worthy. "None of your assault and battery, for I'll undertake to spring the lock."

"Will you so?" said Dr. Johnson, eyeing him thoughtfully.

The watch was no Bow Street constable, but one of the Temple guardians, a stubby old man in a seedy fustian coat, girded with a broad leather belt from which depended his short sword and his truncheon of office.

The women regarded him admiringly as he stepped forward, full of self-importance, and made play with a kind of skewer which he thrust into the lock.

Nothing happened.

After considerable probing and coaxing the man was fain to desist.

" 'Tis plain, sir," he covered his failure, "that the door is bolted from within."

"Bolted!" cried Mrs. Taffety. "Of course 'tis bolted! Mistress Duncom ever barred herself in like a fortress, for she kept a fortune in broad pieces under her bed in a silver tankard, and so she went ever in fear of robbers."

"How came you to know of this fortune, ma'am?" demanded Dr. Johnson.

"Why, sir, the whole world knew, 'twas no secret."

"It ought to have been. Well, fortress or no, it appears we must break in."

"Hold sir!" cried the black-eyed charwoman. "You'll affright the old lady into fits. I know a better way."

"Name it, then, ma'am."

"My master Grisley's chambers, you must know, sir, lie on the other side of the court—"

"Ah, Mr. Grisley!" murmured Aunt Moll. "Pity he's not to the fore, he'd set us right, I warrant, he's that fond of Annet!"

"Mr. Grisley is from home. But I have the key. Now if I get out at his dormer, I'll make my way easily round the parapet, and so get in at Mrs. Duncom's casement and find ou what's amiss."

"Well thought on, Mistress Oliver," approved the watch, "for the benchers of the Temple would take it ill, was we to go banging in doors."

"And how if the casement be bolted and barred, as surely it will be?"

"Then, Mrs. Taffety, I must make shift. Wait here. I'll not be long."

Waiting on the landing, we fell silent, listening for we knew not what. When it came, it startled us—a crash, and the tinkle of falling glass.

"Alack, has she fallen?"

"Not so, ma'am, she has made shift. Now she's within, soon she'll shoot the great bolt and admit us."

We waited at the door in suspense. After an interminable minute, the lock turned, and we heard someone wrenching at the bolt. It stuck; then with a shriek it grated grudgingly back, and the heavy door swung slowly in.

On the threshold stood Mrs. Oliver, rigid and staring. Her lips moved, but no sound came.

"In God's name, what is it?" cried Mrs. Taffety in alarm.

Mrs. Oliver found a hoarse whisper:

"Murder!" she gasped. "Murder lock'd in!"

Her eyes rolled up in her head, her knees gave way, and she collapsed in a huddle in the doorway.

"Let me, sirs." The motherly female stepped forward. "When Katty's in her fits, I know how to deal."

Leaving her to deal, the rest of us pressed in, Dr. Johnson, myself, the watch, and the fluttering women. The Irish girl was with us, but her swains, the sculls, I noted, had vanished.

Wha a sight met our eyes! The young maid's pallet was made up in the passage, by the inner door as if to guard it, and there lay Annet in her blood. She had fought for her life, for blood was everywhere, but repeated blows of an axe or hammer had broke her head and quelled her forever.

In the inner room old Mrs. Duncom lay strangled. The noose was still around her neck. In the other bed old Betty had suffered the same fate. Of the silver tankard there was no trace.

"Murder and robbery! We must send for the Bow Street men!" I cried.

"Not in my bailiwick!" growled the Temple

watchman. "*I* am the law in Bayfield Court!"

"So he is, Mr. Boswell," assented Dr. Johnson. "Well, well, if we put our minds to it, we may make shift to unravel this dreadful riddle for ourselves— three women dead in an apartment locked and barred!"

Cold air touched me and a shudder shook me. The icy air was no ghostly miasma, I soon saw, but a chill spring breeze from the casement, where the small old-fashioned panes nearest the bolt had been shattered when entrance was effected.

"The window was bolted, I told you so!" cried Mrs. Taffety. "Every bolt set! The Devil is in it!"

"The Devil—the Devil!" the charwomen took up the chorus.

"Y'are foolish females!" said the watch stoutly. "Look you, Mr. Johnson, I'll undertake to shew you how 'twas done."

"I thank you, my man—"

"Jona Mudge, sir, at your service."

"I thnk you, honest Mudge, pray instruct me, for I am ever happy to be instructed."

"Then behold, sir! I take this string—" It came out of his capacious pocket with a conjurer's flourish at which the females gaped. "Now pray step this way, sir (leading us to the outer door). Now mark me! I loop my string around the knob of the bolt—I step outside, pray follow—"

On the outside landing Mistress Katty Oliver was sitting propped against the wall with closed eyes, and her friend was assiduously fanning her. They paid us no mind. Lowering his tone, Mudge continued his lecture:

"I bring the two ends of the string with me—I close the door. Now I will pull on both ends of the string, which will shoot the bolt—and so I shall have only to pull away the string by one end, the door is bolted, and I stand outside. As thus—"

As he spoke, he pulled on the two ends of the string. Nothing happened. The unwieldly bolt stuck, and no force applied to the string could budge it.

"An old trick not always to be relied upon," smiled Dr. Johnson. "I thank you, sir, for demonstrating how this strange fear was *not* accomplished!"

As Mudge stood there looking foolish, there was a clatter on the stair, and three gentlemen arrived on the run. The benchers had come back from Commons. Dr. Johnson knew them all, the red-faced one, the exquisite one, the melancholy one, and greeted each in turn.

"What, Mr. Kerry, Mr. Geegan, Mr. Grisley, you come in an unhappy time."

"Your servant, Mr. Johnson, what's amiss?"

Mistress Oliver was on her feet, her hand on his arm.

"Don't go in, Mr. Grisley, for God's sake don't go in. Come away, I'll fetch you a tot, come away."

"Alack, sirs, murder's amiss!" I blurted.

The two young benchers were through the door in an instant, and the melancholy Grisley shook off his maid's hand and followed. When his eye lit on Annet's bloody brow, he cried aloud.

"Cover her face! For God's sake cover her face!"

Quick hands drew up the crimsoned bed-cloathes, and so we found the hammer. Dr. Johnson's shapely strong fingers handled it gingerly, bringing it close to his near-sighted eyes.

"An ordinary hammer. What can it tell us?"

"Perhaps much, for I perceive there's an initial burned in the wood of the handle," said I, feeling pleased with myself. "A G, sir, if I mistake not."

"A G. Yours, Mr. Geegan?"

The exquisite youth jibbed in alarm.

"Not mine, Divil a whit, no, sir, not mine!"

"Mr. Grisley?"

"I cannot look on it, do not ask me. Kat will know."

The little dark woman took his hand and spoke soothingly to him.

"I think sir, 'tis the one you lent to Mr. Kerry some days since."

"To me!" cried the ruddy-faced bencher. "You lie, you trull!"

"I don't lie," said the woman angrily. "Don't you remember, you sent your charwoman for it, I gave it to Biddy to knock in some nails?" In a sudden silence, all eyes turned to the red-haired girl.

"No, sir, I never!" she cried in alarm.

"Go off, you trull!" bawled the alarmed Kerry. "I dismiss you! So you may e'en fetch your bundle and be off with you!"

"Nay, sir, not so fast, she must remain!" remonstrated the watch.

"Not in my chambers, the d—d trull! She may take up her bundle outside my door, and be d—d to her!"

I perceived that Mr. Kerry had come from Commons not a little pot-valiant, and thought it good riddance when he stamped off.

Biddy gave us one scared look, and followed him. Young Geegan seemed minded to go along, but was prevented by the arrival of Mudge's mate of the watch. Leather-belted, truncheon in hand, flat and expressionless of face, there he stood, filling the doorway and saying nothing. It gave us a sinister feeling of being under guard in that chamber of death. Mrs. Taffety fell to sobbing, and the women to comforting her. Dr. Johnson was probing the chimneys, neither deterred nor assisted by the blank-faced watchman, when suddenly Mr. Kerry was back again, redder than ever, hauling a reluctant Biddy by the wrist, and in his free hand brandishing a silver tankard.

" 'Tis Mrs. Duncom's!" cried Mrs. Taffety.

"Hid in Biddy's bundle! I knew it, the trull!"

The wretched Biddy began to snivel.

"I had it for a gift," she wept. "I did not know murder was in it!"

Dr. Johnson took her in hand: "Who gave it you?"

"My f-friends."

"What friends?"

Biddy was loath to say, but the philosopher prevailed by sheer moral force, and Biddy confessed:

"The Sander brothers. Scouts to the benchers. Them that's gone off."

"They shall be found. And what did you do for them?"

"I—" The girl's resistance was broken. "I kept watch on the stair."

Then it came with a rush: "When Annet went in the evening for some wine to make the old lady's nightly posset, she left the door on the jar as was her wont, that she might come in again without disturbing old Betty; and knowing it would be so, Matt Sander, that's the puny one, he slips in and hides under the bed. When all is still, he lets in his brother, and I keep watch on the stair, and they come out with the tankard of broad pieces—" The wretched girl began to bawl. "They swore to me they had done no murder, only bound and gagged the folk for safety's sake."

"And when they came out," pursued Dr. Johnson, "they shot the bolt from outside. How did they do that?"

"I know not what you mean, sir. They pulled the door to, 'tis a spring lock, I heard it snick shut, and so we came away and shared out in the archway below."

"Which of them carried the hammer?"

"Neither, sir, for what would they need a hammer?"

Then realization flooded her, and she bawled louder, looking wildly about for a refuge. Suddenly, defiantly, Mr. Geegan stepped forward and took her in his arms.

"So, Mr. Johnson," said watchman Mudge smugly, "our problem is solved, we had no need of Bow Street! You come along of me, Mistress Biddy. Nay, let go, sir." Mr. Geegan reluctantly obeyed. "Pray, Mr. Johnson, do you remain here, I'll fetch the crowner to sit on the bodies."

"Do so, good friend. I'll desire all those present—" his eye took in the three benchers and the huddling women "—to bear me company till he comes. Bucket will stand by to keep order. Come friends, we shall sit more at our ease in the dining room. After you, ma'am. After you, sir."

They went without demur, all save Grisley. In the passage, by Annet's still form on her pallet, he balked. "Shall she lie alone?" he cried piteously. "I'll stay by her while I may."

"And I by you," said Kat Oliver.

Her master sank to the hallway bench, wringing his hands and crying: "O Annet, Annet, why did you not admit me? I might have saved you!"

"Come, sir," soothed his maid, "be easy, you could do nothing."

We left them fallen silent on the bench. Instead of following the others into the dining room, Dr. Johnson led me back into the inner chamber, where two bodies lay coldly blown upon from the broken window panes.

JOHNSON: There's more in this, Mr. Boswell, than meets the eye.

BOSWELL: Did not the Sanders do it?

JOHNSON: And got out through a door locked and barred, and left it so? Biddy saw no hocussing of the lock, and I question whether they knew how to do it.

BOSWELL: Mudge knew how. Were they in it together? I ask myself, sir, what is this guardian of the Temple peace, that carries a picklock in his pocket, and knows how to shoot a bolt from without? I smell Newgate on him.

JOHNSON: You may be right, sir. They are a queer lot, the Temple watch. But this one is no wizard, he could neither, in the event, pick the lock nor shoot the bolt.

BOSWELL: Then how was it done? This seems an impossible crime.

JOHNSON: 'Twas all too possible, sir, for it happened.

BOSWELL: The women are right, the Devil did it.

JOHNSON: A devil did it indeed, but in human form.

BOSWELL: One who got in through bolts and bars, and got out again leaving all locked and barred behind him?

JOHNSON: There was a way in, for someone got in, and a way out too, that's plain to a demonstration. We must find it

BOSWELL: I am at a loss, sir. Where must we look?

JOHNSON: We must look where all answers are found, sir, in our own heads. Perpend, sir. Murder in a locked dwelling, and no murderer there to take—'tis a pretty mystery, and this one the more complex because it is triple. Let us consider the problem at large. Many answers are possible.

BOSWELL (ruefully): In *my* head, sir, I don't find even one.

JOHNSON: Well, sir, here's one: Perhaps there is no murderer there to take, because there is no murder, only accident that looks like murder.

BOSWELL: Two old women simultaneously strangle themselves by accident, while the young one accidentally falls afoul of a hammer? Come, sir, this is to stretch coincidence and multiply impossibilities!

JOHNSON: Granted, Mr. Boswell. Then is it perhaps double murder and suicide behind bolted doors?

BOSWELL: Suicide by the hammer? Unheard of!

JOHNSON: And nigh on impossible. Well, then, sir, was the tragedy engineered from without, and no murderer ever entered at all?

BOSWELL: The nooses were tightened and the hammer wielded, by someone on the wrong side of the door? This is witchcraft and sorcery, nothing less.

JOHNSON: Then suppose there is no murder, the victim is only stunned or stupefied, until the person who breaks in commits it?

BOSWELL: *Three* murders, sir, and the third a noisy one, all in the one minute while we listened at the door? Come, sir, these conjectures are ingenious, but none fits this case.

JOHNSON: Then there must be a way in, and a way out. Think, Mr. Boswell: all is not so locked and sealed, but holes exist.

BOSWELL: I have it! The keyhole!

JOHNSON: A keyhole that not even a picklock could

penetrate? Think again, sir. What else?

BOSWELL: Nay, I know not, sir. There is no scuttle to the roof.

JOHNSON: There is not, sir.

BOSWELL: And the chimneys are narrow, and stuffed with soot undisturbed.

JOHNSON: So we saw. Not the chimneys. Good. We progress.

BOSWELL: How, progress?

JOHNSON: When one has eliminated all impossibilities, then what remains, however improbable, must be the truth.

BOSWELL: What truth?

JOHNSON: Nay, sir, I have yet to test it. Come with me.

In the passage-way Annet lay still under the reddened blankets. Grisley and his maid sat as still on the settle, he with his face in his hands, she at his shoulder regarding him with a countenance full of concern. A blackened old chair with high back stood opposite. Dr. Johnson ensconced himself therein like some judge on the bench, and I took my stand by him like a bailiff.

"Mistress Oliver," he began, "pray assist our deliberations."

"As best I can, sir," she answered readily.

Grisley did not stir.

"Then tell us, in your airy peregrination, in what condition did you find Mrs. Duncom's casement window?"

"Bolted fast, sir, I was forced to break the glass

that I might reach in and turn the catch."

"I know, we heard it shatter. You broke the glass and reached in. With both hands?"

"Certainly not, sir, I held on with the other hand."

"Then why did you break two panes?"

"I don't know. For greater assurance—"

"Nonsense! I put it to you, my girl, *you found the window broken.*"

"Then why would I break it again?"

"Because you knew at once who had been there before you, and thought only to shield him. So you broke the second pane, that we might hear the crash of glass, and think you had been forced to break in. The broken window would else tell us that the murderer came from Mr. Grisley's casement."

"He never!" cried the woman, on her feet before her master as if to shield him. "Would he kill Annet, that he lusted after?"

"Would he not, if she resisted him? These violent passions have violent ends. No, no. I pity him, but justice must be done. Think, Mistress Oliver, this is the man that slunk around the parapet at dead of night, a hammer in his pocket. With it he breaks a pane, turns the bolt, and enters. The two helpless old women fall victim to his string, lest they hinder his intent. When Annet resists him, in his fury he batters her to death, and so flees as he came. May such a creature live?"

This harangue slowly penetrated the mind of the unhappy Grisley, and he rose to his feet.

"Bucket!" called Dr. Johnson sharply. The watchman appeared. "Take him in!"

"No! No!" cried the woman. "He is innocent!"

"Who will believe it?" countered Johnson. "No, ma'am, he'll hang for it, and justly too. Did you ever see a man hanged, Mr. Boswell? It is a shocking sight to see a man struggling as he strangles in a string, his face suffused, his limbs convulsed, for long horrible minutes. Well, he has earned it. Take him, Bucket."

As Bucket collared the unresisting Grisley, we found we had a fury on our hands. With nails and teeth Kat Oliver fell upon Dr. Johnson. I had her off in a trice; but I could not have held her had not Bucket come to my aid.

"I thank you, Mr. Boswell," said Dr. Johnson, settling his neckcloth and staunching his cheek, "your address has saved me a mauling. A woman's a lioness in defence of what she loves."

"In my belief she's mad," said I angrily, as the wiry little woman wrenched against our pinioning arms.

"That may also be true. A thin line divides great love and madness. Give over, ma'am, let justice take its course. So, that's better—let her go, Mr. Boswell. As to Mr. Grisley, Bucket, to Newgate with him, and lock him in the condemned cell."

"You shan't! You shan't!" sobbed Kat Oliver wildly. "It was I that killed them, it was I, it was I!"

"You, ma'am? A likely story! Why would you do such a thing?"

"Why would I destroy that prim little bitch, that was destroying him? For his sake, gladly. Yet I never meant to use the hammer, that I carried only to break the glass—"

"But," I objected, "Biddy had the hammer!"

"You are deceived, Mr. Boswell. To disclaim the hammer, this woman did not scruple to lie. Well, then, Mrs. Oliver, if not to use the hammer, what was your intent?"

The little woman's eyes looked inward, and she spoke with a kind of horrid relish:

"When I knew the people lay bound and gagged—"

"How did you know?"

"I heard the talk on the landing. I could not sleep for thinking of—I could not sleep, and the boys were drunk and loud. I opened the door and listened. I saw my opportunity. How I entered you know. The old women I finished neatly, with their own curtain cords. The young one—"

"Yes, the young one?"

"The young one I reserved for a more dreadful fate. It was I who shot the front-door bolt, intending to leave her locked in with murder, and see her hanged for it."

"Who could think she did it, when she lay bound?" I demanded.

"Of course I did away with the bonds," said the woman contemptuously.

"Yet you killed her, how was that to your purpose?"

"I meant only to stun her, but she got loose and fought me. I saw red. I killed her. Then I returned as I came."

"And when the people became alarmed and would break in," Dr. Johnson supplied, "you saw it must be you, and no one else, to break the window and effect an entrance there, lest the broken window be observed by others, pointing directly at the folk from Mr. Grisley's."

She made no answer, but turned to her master.

"I did it for you, Edward."

With a blind gesture, Grisley turned away.

"All for nothing, then."

Dining together the next day at the Mitre, we naturally turned our talk to the exciting hours we had spent in Bayfield Court the day before.

BOSWELL: Were you not surprised, sir, when Katty Oliver confessed her guilt?

JOHNSON: Not at all, sir, I knew it all along. What did she care if the door was battered in? Only the strongest of motives would suffice to set her on that precarious circuit she traversed. She must have known what would be found at the end of it. Nay, more, how did she know it was an easy way around the parapet, if she had not traversed it before?

BOSWELL: Yet how eloquently you depicted the unhappy Grisley's crime and his imminent fate.

JOHNSON: Thus I put her to the torture, for I could see how much he meant to her; and when I turned the screw with talk of the horrors of hanging, she confessed to save him, as I foresaw she would.

BOSWELL: What will become of her? Surely she'll hang?

JOHNSON: In the ordinary course, sir, yes. But I had the curiosity to enquire this morning, and by what I learn, she will not hang. It appears that, as Aunt Moll said, she was ever subject to fits, no doubt she committed her terrible crimes in an unnatural phrenzy. Well, sir, when she saw the cells last night she fell into a dead catalepsy and was carried insensible to Bedlam, where 'tis clear she belongs.

BOSWELL: And Biddy, what of her?

JOHNSON: The Sander brothers, that delivered over the old women bound to be murdered, have made good their escape, leaving Biddy to pay for their crime.

BOSWELL: This seems unfair, sir.

JOHNSON: Why, sir, receiving of stolen goods is a hanging offence, Miss Biddy cannot complain. But the Temple watchmen are not incorruptible, and the Temple watch-house is not impregnable. Moreover, Mr. Geegan, the son of an Irish Peer, has well-lined pockets. In short, sir, he has spirited away Miss Biddy, who knows whither. And so ends the affair of murder lock'd in.

BOSWELL (boldly): Which I hope I may one day narrate at large when, as I mean to do, I record for posterity the exploits of *Sam: Johnson, detector!*

✝

[The hardest thing about writing this story was making it probable. I suppose this is because it actually happened. Real events don't necessarily bother about probability.

It happened, and I tell it as it happened, except of course for the intervention of Dr. Sam: Johnson. The solution is my own. In actual fact the Irish girl was hanged, which seems hard for only keeping watch and accepting a silver tankard, but such was justice in those inhuman days.

In analyzing the "locked-room mystery" and its possible solutions, with singular prescience Dr. Johnson seems to have anticipated John Dickson Carr's "locked-room lecture" in *The Three Coffins*; though the solution that detector Sam: Johnson arrives at is not among those considered by Carr.

The classic "string trick" for bolting a door from outside, here explained by the watchman, was actually demonstrated at the Irish girl's trial, when they brought the door into open court and performed the trick upon it to the amazement of all beholders. You may real all about it in George Borrow's *Celebrated Trials* (New York : Payson & Clarke, Ltd., 1928) II, 536-571.

Why, you may ask, do I write "Sam: Johnson?" Because that's how he wrote it. So he signed himself. The colon in his day, as the period in ours, indicated an abbreviation. His full name was Samuel.]

THE BEDLAM BAM

"To find my Tom o' Bedlam ten thousand miles I'll travel," chanted the ballad-singer in a thin rusty screech, lustily seconded by the wail of the dirt-encrusted baby in her shawl.

"Mad Maudlin goes with dirty toes to save her shoes from gravel.

Yet will I sing bonny mad boys, Bedlam boys are bonny,

They still go bare and live by air . . ."

All along the fence that separated Bedlam Hospital from the tree-lined walks of Moorfields, ill-printed broadsides fluttered in the breeze, loudly urged upon the public by a cacophony of ballad-sellers. As I flinched at the din, a hand plucked my sleeve, and a voice twittered:

"Poor Tom o' Bedlam! Tom's a-cold!"

I turned to view a tatterdemalion figure, out at elbow and knee, out at toe and heel, out at breech, with spiky hair on end and claw-like hand extended. As I fumbled for a copper, my wise companion restrained me.

"Let be, Mr. Boswell, the man's a fraud. No Bedlamite has leave to beg these days; they are all withinside. Come along."

Leaving the mock madman to mutter a dispirited curse, we passed through Bedlam gate and approached the noble edifice, so like a palace without, so grim within—as I, a visitor from North Britain, was soon to learn.

Behold us then mounting the step to the entrance pavilion. If "great wits are sure to madness near allied," as the poet has it, then what shall be said of that ill-assorted pair?—Dr. Sam: Johnson, the Great Cham of Literature, portly of mien and rugged of countenance, with myself, his young friend and chronicler, James Boswell, advocate, of Scotland, swarthy of complection and low of stature beside him. Believing London to be the full tide of human existence, he had carried me, that day in May 1768, to see one of the city's strangest sights, Bedlam Hospital, the abode of the frantick and the melancholy mad.

Entering the pavilion, we beheld before us the Penny Gates, attended by a burly porter in blue coat and cap, wearing with importance a silver badge almost as wide as a plate, and holding his silver-tipped staff of office. Beside the flesh and blood figure stood two painted wooden effigies holdings jugs, representing gypsies, a he and a she. Though the woman was ugly, we put our pennies into her jug, and heard them rattle down; whereupon the porter passed us in, and we ascended to the upper gallery.

As we came out on the landing, our senses were assailed by a rank stench and a babel of noise, a hum of many voices talking, with an accompaniment of screech and howl that stood my hair on end.

A second blue-gowned attendant passed us through the iron bars of the barrier, and we stood in the long gallery of the men's ward. Around us milled madmen and their visitors in a dense throng, the while vendors shouldered their way through the crush dispensing nuts, fruits, and cheesecakes, and tap-boys rushed pots of beer, though contraband, to the thirsty, whether mad or sane.

Along the side gallery, tall windows let in the north light. Opposite them were ranged the mad-men's cells, each with its heavy door pierced with a little barred Judas window. Some doors were shut; but more were open to afford the inmates air. I peeped in the first one with a shudder. A small, unglazed window high up admitted a shaft of sun-light and a blast of cold spring air. For furnishings, there was only a wooden bed-stead piled with straw, and a wooden bowl to eat from; unless you counted a heavy iron chain with a neck loop, stapled to the wall. No one was chained there, however; the fortu-nate occupants had "the liberty of the corridor," and perhaps stood at my elbow.

Others were not so fortunate. As we strolled for-ward, we saw through the open doors many a wretch in fetters, chained to the wall, and many a hopeless mope drearily staring.

"Here in Bedlam," remarked my philosophical friend, "tho' secluded from the world, yet we may see the world in microcosm. Here's Pride—"

I looked where he pointed. Through the open door of the next cell, I perceived one who in his disordered intellect imagined himself to be, perhaps, the Great Mogul. He sat on straw as on a throne, he wore his fetters like adornments, and his countenance bore the most ineffable look of self-satisfaction and consequence. For a crown he wore his chamber pot.

"A pride scarce justified," said I with a smile.

"For mortal man, pride is never justified. Here's Anger—"

The sound of blows rang through the corridor. In the neighbouring cell, a red-faced lunatick was furiously beating the straw on his pallet.

"What do you, friend?" enquired a stander-by.

"I beat him for his cruelty!"

"Whom do you beat, sir?"

"The Butcher Duke of Cumberland. Take that! And that!"

"Madmen have long memories," remarked my friend with pity. "The cruelties of the '45 are gone by these twenty years."

The noise had stirred up the menagerie. Pandemonium burst forth. Those who were fettered clanked their chains. Those who were locked in shook the bars. Some howled like wolves. Keepers banging on doors added to the hollobaloo. My friend shuddered.

"God keep us out of such a place!"

"Amen!" said I.

The tumult abated, and we walked on through the throng. A little way along, my friend greeted an acquaintance:

"What, Lawyer Trevelyan, your servant, sir. Miss Cicely, yours. Be acquainted with my young friend Mr. Boswell, the Scotch lawyer, who visits London to see the sights with me."

As I bowed I took their measure. The lawyer was tall and sturdy, with little shrewd eyes in a long closed-up face. The girl was small and slim, modestly attired in dove grey. At her slender waist, in the old-fashioned way, she wore a dainty seamstress' hussif with a business-like pair of scissors suspended on a ribband. Her quiet face was gently framed by a cap and lappets of lawn. Meeting her candid amber gaze, I was glad I had adorned my person in my gold-laced scarlet coat.

"How do you go on, Mr. Trevelyan? And how does the good man, your uncle Silas, the Turkey merchant?"

"On his account, Dr. Johnson, we are come hither."

"What, is he confined here?"

"Alas, yes. Yonder he stands."

I looked where he pointed. The elder Mr. Trevelyan was a wiry small personage, clad in respectable black. He had a thin countenance, his own white hair to his shoulders, bright black eyes, and a risible look. With a half smile, he listened to the tirade of a distrest fellow inmate, giving now and then a quick nod.

"He has no look of insanity," observed my friend.

"Perhaps not, sir. But the prank that brought him hither was not sane. You shall hear. Being touched with Mr. Wesley's *enthusiasm*—"

"Mr. Wesley is a good man."

"I do not deny it, sir. But my uncle has more zeal than prudence. He abandons his enterprises, and goes about to do good to the poor, in prisons and work-houses and I know not where."

"Call you this lunacy?"

"No, sir. Stay, you shall hear the story. Of a Sunday, sir, he gets up into the pulpit at St. Giles, just as the congregation is assembled. He wears a pair of large muslin wings to his shoulders, and 'Follow me, good people!' he cries. 'Follow me to Heaven!' Whereupon with jerks of his hands he flaps his wings, crows loudly, and prepares to launch himself from the lectern. But the beadle, a man of prompt address, pulls him back, and so he is hustled hither without more ado, and here he must stay lest he do himself a mischief. But never fret, Cicely, I have his affairs well in hand, by power of attorney and so on."

But Cicely had gone impulsively to the old gentleman.

"How do you, uncle?"

"Why, my dear, very well. Reflect (smiling) 'tis

only in Bedlam a man may speak his mind about kings and prelates without hindrance. And where else can a man find so many opportunities for comforting the afflicted?"

"Yet, dear uncle, it distresses me to see you among them."

"Be comforted, Cicely. 'Tis only a little while, and I shall be enlarged, I promise you. Your cousin Ned will see to it."

A wise wink accompanied this assurance. Cousin Ned sighed.

"All in good time, Cicely."

Since Cicely seemed minded to canvass the subject further, we bowed and retired. The morning was drawing to a close. I was glad to leave the whole scene of madness, and return to the world of the sane.

Nor would I willingly have renewed my visit so soon, had not the dove-grey girl come to us in distress and urgently carried us thither to visit her uncle.

What a change was there! Two weeks before, we had seen him fully cloathed and quite composed. Now as we peeped through the Judas windows, we beheld him lying on straw in the chilly cell, his shirt in tatters, his white locks tangled, shackled and manacled to the floor.

"A violent case," said the burly mad-keeper. "I dare not unlock the door."

He dared after all, but only upon receipt of a

considerable bribe, and upon condition that he stand
by the door with staff in hand.

In a trice Miss Cicely was kneeling by her uncle's
side, putting her own cloak about him.

"Alas, how do you, uncle?"

The eyes he turned upon her were clear and sane.

"Why, very well, dear love," he said, "I have
learned what I came here to learn, and more too," he
added wryly.

"What have you learned, uncle?"

"I have learned how the poor madmen here are
abused, aye and beaten too, when their poor addled
wits make them obstreperous. That staff (nodding
towards the blue-coat by the door) is not only for
shew."

"Alack, uncle, have you been beaten?"

"Beaten? Aye, and blistered, physicked,
drenched with cold water, denied my books, deprived of pen, ink, and paper. And all for a transport
of justifiable anger."

"Anger at what?" enquired Dr. Johnson.

"At my nephew."

"Why, uncle, what has Ned done?"

"Ned has cozened me. You must know, Dr.
Johnson, I am as well in my wits as you are—save for
my ill judgement in trusting Ned. You see, sir, Mr.
Wesley and his followers are barred from visiting
Newgate Gaol—lest they corrupt the inmates, I
suppose—and from Bedlam Hospital, lest they
make them mad. Well, sir, being determined to
know how matters went on behind these doors when

they are closed, I resolved to make myself an inmate. I gave Ned—more fool me—my power of attorney and a letter that should enlarge me when I so desired, and by enacting a little comedy, with muslin wings, I got myself brought hither; in full confidence that Ned would see me released when I chose."

"Well, sir?"

"Well, sir, when I gave Ned the word to produce my letter and release me, this Judas Iscariot looks me in the eye, and says he, 'What letter? The poor man is raving.' All came clear in a flash. Ned has no intention of enlarging me. Why should he, when he has my power of attorney, and may make ducks and drakes of my fortune at his pleasure? Nay, he is my heir. What are my chances, think you, of coming out of here alive? Do you wonder I was ready to throttle the scoundrel? But they pulled me from him, and I have been chained down ever since. The keepers are bribed, I suppose. To my expostulations they turn a deaf ear. If not for Cicely, my plight need never have been known."

"Alack, Dr. Johnson," cried Cicely, "now what's to be done?"

"Have no fear, my dear. When next the Governors of the hospital meet, they shall hear the story, and he'll be released, I warrant you."

That very Saturday at nine of the lock we presented ourselves in the Court Room of the hospital. This handsome chamber is located abovestairs in the central pavilion, a gracious room with large windows overlooking Moorfields, a ceiling of carven plaster, and painted coats of arms about the walls.

Here sat the Governors, a stately set of men in full wigs and wide-skirted coats. My eye picked out Dr. John Monro, head surgeon, a formidable figure with bushy eyebrows, a belligerent snub nose, a short upper lip over prominent dog-teeth, a vinous complection, and a bulldog cast of countenance; for upon his say-so, in the end, depended our friend's freedom or incarceration.

Four of us came to speak for him that morning: James Boswell, lawyer, Dr. Johnson, his friend, and Miss Cicely, his kinswoman. To strengthen our ranks, we brought a medical man, Dr. Robert Levet, Dr. Johnson's old friend, who for twenty years had dwelt in his house and attended him at need. He was a little fellow of grotesque and uncouth appearance, his knobby countenance half concealed by a bushy wig. He wore a voluminous rusty black coat, and old-fashioned square-toed shoes to his feet. Thus ceremoniously attired, he came with us to speak as a physician in support of Mr. Silas Trevelyan's sanity.

Then they brought him in, and my heart misgave me. Gaunt, ragged, in chains, with his white hair on end—was this man sane? At his benevolent greeting to us, however, and his respectful bow to the committee assembled, I took heart again. As the blue-coated warders ranged themselves beside him, for fear of some disorderly outbreak, the gentlemen seated along the dais scanned him intently, and he looked serenely back.

Footsteps hurrying up the stair announced yet another participant, and nephew Edward Trevelyan appeared precipitately in the wide doorway—heir, attorney, and nearest of kin to the supposed madman, all in one.

The proceedings began. Dr. Johnson was eloquent, Dr. Levet earnest and scientifick, Miss Cicely modest and low-spoken. I was furnished forth with legal instances. Our one difficulty was in explaining how, if he was sane, our friend had gotten himself into Bedlam in the first place. We dared not say, in effect, "He came in voluntarily, as a spy." We skirted the subject, and concentrated upon his present state of restored sanity.

"We have now," said Dr. Monro, "only to hear from Mr. Edward Trevelyan, the inmate's attorney and kinsman. Mr. Trevelyan?"

Cousin Ned unfolded his length, rolled up his little eyes, and spoke softly in a deep resonant voice:

"Grieved I am to say it," he began, "my friends over there mistake my poor uncle's condition. He can be sly and plausible, sirs, but with me, whom he trusts"—old Mr. Trevelyan stiffened, and Cicely put a dismayed hand to her mouth—"with me he speaks otherwise. His brain still swarms with lunatick fancies. He proposes to get upon the roof and with his wings elude them all, and a good job too, says he, for the Governor is a puppy that wants a cannister to his tail, and Dr. Monro is a cork-brained clunch—"

With a roar the uncle broke from his keepers and flung himself upon his nephew.

"Thou prevaricating pup! Thou lying leech! Thou Judas! Where is my letter that I gave thee for my safety?"

"The man is mad," growled Dr. Monro. "Take him away, and let him be close confined."

We four met again next morning for breakfast in Johnson's Court. We shared a loaf, and little Levet brewed pot after pot of tea, for which Dr. Johnson's capacity was vast.

"And now," pronounced Dr. Johnson, setting down his cup at last, "what's to be done next for our incarcerated friend, Mr. Silas Trevelyan? He cannot stay where he is. Chains and fetters would soon drive the sanest man mad."

"If we could perswade the keepers he is sane?" suggested Miss Cicely timidly.

"After Dr. Monro's verdict," said I, "how can we so? We can never get him away openly."

"Then we must bring him away covertly," said Dr. Johnson. "Can you not, Mr. Boswell, devise some bam that shall bamboozle the keepers and set Mr. Silas free?"

"Let me think. What do you say, sir, if we take a leaf from Shakespeare, and deliver our friend, like Falstaff, in a buckingbasket of foul linen?"

"Chain and all?"

"True, there's the chain."

"Take a leaf from *Romeo and Julet*, and they'll undo the chain fast enough, I warrant you," mused little Levet.

Johnson frowned; then smiled: "We'll try it."

Accordingly we spent the best part of the day concerting our measures and assembling our properties. As the afternoon wore on, our physician was furnished forth with a bagful of flasks and vials, clean linen, and money to spend, and so departed for Bedlam to acquaint Mr. Silas with our plan, and put things in motion. We set our rendezvous there for midnight.

Punctually at midnight, we two, escorting Miss, drove up to Bedlam gate in a hackney coach. A cart followed us, with a large pine box for freight. Instructing our Jehu to stand, we rang the porter's bell. That functionary presently appeared, rubbing sleep from his eyes.

We soon saw that our precursor had opened the way for us by his authority as a medical man, plus, I doubt not, a judicious outlay of cash bribes. When we named our stricken friend, Mr. Silas Trevelyan, the fellow looked grave, passed us up the stair, and went yawning back to his hole.

At the barred gate on the landing, a second blue-coated warder was ready with the keys. They hung by a loop at his broad leather belt. As he selected and turned the right one, I scrutinized him narrowly, for upon his behavior depended, in part, the success of our scheam.

The fellow was tall and muscular, as befitted one who was often called upon to grapple with lunaticks. Little squinting eyes in a broad doughy face gave him a look more dogged than quick. True to his looks, he dogged us close as we entered the ward.

The long shadowy corridor was empty; the mad-men had all been sequestered for the night. Eerie noises attested to their presence behind the locked doors: a snore and a snort here, a patter of prayer there, an occasional howl or screech of laughter that shocked the ear.

One door only was open, whence faint candle light fell along the floor. Dr. Levet stood in the doorway.

"Be brave, my dear," said he to Cicely, taking her hand. "He is very far gone, and turning black. He has sent for you, only to give you his last blessing. Stand back, fellow (to the mad-keeper), these moments are sacred."

The warder, looking solemn, took up his stance by the door, and we passed within. Our friend Mr. Silas lay on his straw pallet, his eyes turned up in his head. Out of respect for his obviously moribund condition, his chains had been removed.

As Dr. Levet advanced the candle and pushed back the tangled locks, I saw the awful leaden blackness of the skin. Had I not been prepared for it, I should have been shocked. Even prepared, Miss Cicely clung to my hand as she whispered:

"How do you, uncle?"

The dark eyes came into focus upon her.

"Ill, ill, my dear," he breathed. "The lawyer—is he here?"

"I am here, sir."

"Then write my last will—quickly. To my niece—every thing to my niece."

His head dropped back. Dr. Levet held a draught to his lips. I drew forth my tablets and wrote down his bequest the briefest way. Faltering fingers signed it, and Dr. Johnson added his firm neat signature as witness.

"Take it, Cicely," murmured the testator. She slipped it into her bodice. "And," the failing voice continued, "may Heaven bless you. I forgive—"

The voice died, the white head dropped back, the jaw fell. Dr. Levet touched the slack wrist. Swiftly he closed the eyelids and drew the sheet over the darkened face.

"Our friend is no more," he pronounced gravely.

"What, dead?" ejaculated the mad-keeper, starting forward.

"Stand back!" cried Dr. Levet. "On your life, stand back! Such a death has not been these hundred years in England, for our friend is dead of the Black Plague! Look at his face—"

He flicked back the sheet and momentarily by the pale light of the candle revealed the blackened countenance; at which the mad-keeper started back with an oath.

"Now hark'ee, my friend," began Dr. Johnson

portentously, "be guided by me: were this known, there would be rioting within these walls; what keeper would be safe? Do you but keep silence, all shall be decently done by us, his friends. He shall be gone by morning, and the episode forgotten. Nor shall you be the loser," he added, fingering his pocket suggestively.

The fellow was stupid, which suited us; but so stupid that precious moments went past while we strove to make him see the supposed seriousness of the situation. Not so another keeper, a dark-visaged fellow with a squint who happened by. Hearing that Mr. Silas Trevelyan had but now died of the Black Death, he at once clapped a dirty handkerchief to his nose, and clattered off down the stair.

The first fellow was still mumbling when Dr. Levet settled the matter. He advanced the candle, clapped a hand to the fellow's face, and cried out:

"What, friend! 'Tis too late! You have taken the infection! You are all of a sweat, and turning black! (And so he was, glistening with ink from Levet's hand.) A clyster! Only a clyster will save you now! This way! To your own quarters!"

Speaking thus urgently, the physician steered the terrified fellow in the direction of his lair in the attick. We were left to do the last offices for the "dead," who lay motionless, looking more risible now than ever.

The supposed corpse was neatly laid out, cocooned in his winding sheet, when Dr. Levet appeared in the gallery alone, chuckling.

"A good strong enema—that will take care of the keeper," said he with a grin. "He'll be busy for a while. Come, let us go."

"Go!" cried Dr. Johnson. "Without the keeper, how are we to make our way through the barriers?"

"With his keys," said Levet, and produced them. "A clyster is a powerfully distracting operation. 'Twas child's play to get at the keys, though under his nose."

"Well done, Mr. Levet. Come, let us go."

Among us we made shift to carry the sheeted body through the barred gate, down the wide stair, and out at the portal, which the largest key unlocked, not without an alarming screech. A snore from the porter's lodge gave us Godspeed. Dawn light was greying the sky as we lifted our burden into the waiting cart. We eased the sheeted figure into the pine coffin. I lowered the lid, and Dr. Johnson screwed it lightly down.

"—in case we encounter the curious. 'Tis but until we get clear of the grounds," he reassured his friend in an undertone.

I noted with approval that underneath the bow of crape that mournfully adorned the lid, auger holes had been bored to provide the "corpse" air to breathe.

The carter, a scrawny pock-marked boy, was regarding our proceedings between alarm and superstitious awe.

"Is he dead? I'll have no part in it! Give me my money and get him out of my cart!"

By paying a double fee, we managed to retain the cart; but the carter took to his heels. I must perforce take the reins. Miss elected to share my lot. She could not be perswaded to leave her uncle in my hands, but sat herself determinedly upon his coffin. Dr. Johnson and Mr. Levet mounted the hackney coach without us.

We had wasted precious time. Before we could drive off, we were intercepted. Two fellows came up at the run. One wore the blue coat of a mad-keeper. I recognized the swarthy keeper who had sheered off so quickly. Now it became clear: the fellow was one of Ned's tools, and had run off, not to shun infection, but to inform; for his companion was Ned.

"Alas, my uncle!" said the false, mellifluous voice. "Why was I not notified? As his heir—"

"We have performed the last offices," said Dr. Johnson coldly from the coach, "and you shall hear further. We'll not bandy words at Bedlam gate. Drive on, Mr. Boswell."

I drove on.

How it fell out I know not, but I missed my rendezvous in the leafy walks of Moorfields. It was not the coach that overtook me, but a pair of footpads coming suddenly out of the shadows.

"Stand and deliver!"

A weapon glinted, and a rough hand pulled me from the high seat.

"Stay, you mistake," I cried; "here is no treasure chest—"

But the two fellows were up and slapping the

reins, and off they went, cart and coffin and Miss and all; and as I stood dumbfounded, there floated back to me the girl's despairing cry:

"Cousin Ned!"

Here was calamity indeed. I could think of no better plan than to bellow "Stop thief!" which I did with a will. Wheels crunched on gravel, and the coach drew up beside me. Little Levet reached a hand and pulled me inside.

When he had heard my story, Dr. Johnson looked utterly grave.

"What have we done? We have delivered our friend, out of Bedlam indeed, straight into the hands of his enemy!"

"And his heir!" exclaimed Dr. Levet.

"No, sir." I corrected him. "Recall, sir, that as part of the comedy of the 'death bed,' I made his will. 'Every thing to my niece.' The girl is his heir."

"But does her venal cousin know that?"

"She knows it," said Levet wryly. "She need not lift a finger. She has only to let him be buried, and his fortune is hers."

"Great Heavens!" I cried. "That innocent face!"

"Innocent faces have masked murderous hearts before now." mused Dr. Johnson. "*Vide* Mary Blandy, *vide* your own Katharine Nairn."

"I'll never believe it," said I stoutly.

"Believe it or no, we must act to save him, and quickly."

"The more quickly," said Levet urgently, "that in too slavish imitation of *Romeo and Juliet*, I have made him helpless with a sleeping draught."

"Thus, then, the matter stands," Johnson summed up. "The lawyer thinks himself the heir. Perhaps he supposes he is in possession of his uncle's corpse. If so, he will bury him, thus rendering him a corpse indeed. Perhaps he has unscrewed the coffin lid and found a sleeping man. What is to hinder him from quietly doing away with him? Either way, he looks to inherit."

"And perhaps he is in concert with Miss, they'll bury him and split the swag," suggested Levet.

I shook my head vehemently.

"We must find him," said Dr. Johnson. "There is one hope yet. No one at all will inherit, if the old gentleman is not known to be dead. They cannot inter him secretly. Come, let us make inquiries. They all dwell together in a house in Jasper Street. To Jasper Street, coachman."

Jasper Street was nearby. There all was silent. No cart stood before the door, but as we stood knocking, a manservant trudged up. He stared.

"Han't you heard? I have just carried the news to our nearest friends. The master is dead of a mighty infection. They daren't keep him. His sermon will be preached as soon as may be, and so they'll put him hastily under ground."

"Where, friend?"

"At the parish church, where else, St. Giles Cripplegate."

Without further parley we drove off in haste. As we turned into the street called London Wall, we heard the great bell of St. Giles begin to toll. A few moments more, and we were there. The east transept door was nearest, and we entered in haste. A charnelhouse smell seemed to taint the dusky air. It emanated from the opened vault before the Trevelyan monument, where soon the deceased must be inhumed.

Was he deceased? Within that plain pine coffin forward in the aisle, sleeping or waking, did he still live? Could we bring him off alive from this peril we had put him in?

My eye sought the chief mourner where he sat in his forward pew. Nephew Ned wore a black mourning cloak, and made play with a large cambrick handkerchief. Miss was not beside him.

Then I saw her, kneeling at the coffin foot in her dove-grey gown, clinging with both hands to the edge. As I looked, the sexton tried to detach her from this unseemly pose, but she shook her head and clung.

From the pulpit the sermon was already flowing over us in a glutinous tide. The deceased was a mirror of all the works of mercy, visiting the sick, the imprisoned, the distracted, and now gone to his reward in the blessed hope of the resurrection,

"For verily he shall rise again—"

Miss Cicely stood up suddenly. A long creaking rasp set my teeth on edge as the coffin lid was slowly pushed up, and a sheeted figure rose to a sitting position.

The parson gabbled a prayer, ladies shrieked, and

Lawyer Trevelyan uttered a most unseemly curse.

Helped by Cicely, the supposed corpse put back his cerements and bowed to the startled company.

"I thank you, reverend sir," said Mr. Silas coolly, "for your good opinion, and you, my friends, for paying me my honours, tho' prematurely. 'Tis too long a tale, how I came hither thus. Suffice it to say, I am neither dead nor mad, and I desire you will all join me at my house to break fast in celebration. You, nephew, need not come. You'll hear from me later. But you, dear niece, give me your hand. Come, friends, let us go."

So saying, in his madman's rags as he was, wearing his winding-sheet like a cloak, handing Miss Cicely, he led the way down the center aisle. We fell in behind him, and so the strange procession came to the house in Jasper Street. There the dumbfounded servants served the old gentleman his own funeral baked meats (hastily fetched from the nearby tavern).

Only when the general company had dispersed did we learn the full story of those hours between the time the coffin was stolen by nephew Ned, and the time we found it lying in the church to be preached over.

"The rattling of the cart awoke me," said old Trevelyan, "for your sleeping draught, sir (to Dr. Levet), was not so very strong. When I heard my nephew's voice, I knew my situation was precarious indeed. I kept silence, only thanking Dr. Johnson for his foresight in screwing down the lid."

"What is screwed may be unscrewed," remarked Dr. Johnson, "that was the most of my concern."

"That it was not," said Mr. Silas, "we may thank this brave girl here. She sat upon the lid, and would not stir, and between seeming stubborn grief and the menace of infection, she kept her cousin at a distance. She never budged from my side. Only after Ned had left my coffin in the aisle and was gone to instruct the parson and the sexton, did I hear the screws turn in the lid."

"How, with what, then, Miss Cicely, did you make shift to turn them?" asked Dr. Johnson.

"The scissors of a hussif, sir, have more use than snipping thread. But, sir," she went on, with a smile that irradiated her quiet face, "I dared not lift the lid while my cousin ruled. I still clung tight to the coffin, hoping, sir (to Dr. Johnson), for your arrival to protect us. When I saw you in the doorway, I whispered, 'Now, uncle—' and the rest you know."

"A very pretty resurrection scene," remarked my friend with a smile.

" 'Tis not every man," added Mr. Trevelyan, "that lives to hear his own eulogy preached. I am your debtor, sir (to Dr. Levet), for that privilege. To you, gentlemen three, I owe my liberty; and to you, dear Cicely, having fallen into Ned's hands, I am well assured I owe my life. I have made you my heir in a mummery, my dear: you shall be so in earnest."

[In Dr. Sam: Johnson's day, it was still a fashionable amusement to visit Bethlehem Hospital and laugh at the lunatics; and the philosopher once made such an excursion with his young friend Boswell, though certainly not to laugh.

The lot of the madman in Bedlam is here described as depicted by many contemporary writers and artists, notably Hogarth. For more about Bedlam, see F. O. O'Donoghue, *The Story of Bethlehem Hospital* (London: T. Fisher Unwin, 1914).

The prime mover in the fictitious "bam" (short for "bamboozle"), Dr. Robert Levet, Johnson's friend and inmate, comes straight out of Boswell's *Life of Johnson*. The character of Old Trevelyan owes something to real reformers like John Howard; otherwise he and his kin are fictitious.]

THE DISAPPEARING
SERVANT WENCH

Elizabeth Canning went from her Friends between nine and ten on *Monday* Night, being New Year's Night; betwixt *Houndsditch & Bishopsgate*, fresh-colour'd, pitted with ye Small-pox, high Forehead, light Eyebrows, about five foot high, well-set, had on a purple masquerade stuff Gown, black stuff Petticoat, a white Chip Hat bound round with green, white Apron and Handkerchief, blue Stockings, and leather Shoes. Any Coachman, who remembers taking up such a Person, and can give any Account where she is, shall have Two Guineas Reward, to be paid by Mrs. *Canning*, in *Aldermanbury Postern*, Sawyer, which will greatly satisfy her Mother.

These lines were roughly printed in the form of a handbill. My friend Dr. Sam: Johnson, *detector* of crime and chicane, produced the dog's-eared scrap of paper from the accumulations in his untidy book-garret in his house in Johnson's Court. I perused it with care.

"Pray, sir," I ventured, "have you still, in April,

hopes of finding the girl? Sure the thing is all too plain. The lass has been caught up and carried off by some rakish fellow, and now ten to one she plies a shameful trade by Covent Garden, and shames to return to her mother."

"No, sir, there you are out. The girl has returned to her home long since."

"Why then, sir, the girl has told her tale, and there's an end on't."

"Yes, sir, the girl has told her tale indeed, and thence arises the puzzle."

"Pray tell it me."

"Why, thus sir: 'Twas King Charles's Martyrdom Eve, eight and twenty days after that fatal New Year's Day, and the sawyer's 'prentice was just upon locking the door for the night, when there comes a faint knocking. 'Tis Elizabeth Canning! She is sodden, and starving, and exhausted and blue, and her cloathes are gone. Good lack, cries Goody Canning, Bet, what has happened to you? And Bet tells her tale. Stay, you shall hear it as she told it in Bow Street."

From a mass of old printed papers my bulky friend drew a thin pamphlet, and from it began to read out in his sonorous voice:

"The INFORMATION *of Elizabeth Canning of Aldermanbury Postern, London,* Spinster.

"This Informant, upon her Oath, saith, that on Monday, the First Day of January last past, she, this Informant, went to see her Uncle and Aunt, who live at Salt-Petre Bank, near Rosemary-Lane, in the County of Middlesex, and continued with them until the Evening; and saith, That upon her Return home, about Half an Hour after Nine, being opposite Bethlehem-gate in Moorfields, she, this Informant, was seized by two men (whose Names are unknown to her, this Informant) who both had brown Bob-wigs on, and drab-coloured Great-coats; one of whom held her, this Informant, whilst the other, feloniously and violently, took from her one Shaving Hat, one Stuff Gown, and one Linen Apron, which she had on; and also, Half a Guinea in Gold, and three Shillings in Silver; and then he that held her threatened to do for this Informant. And this Informant saith, That, immediately after, they, the same two Men, violently took hold of her, and dragged her up into the Gravel-walk that leads down to the said Gate, and about the Middle thereof he the said Man, that first held her, gave her, with his Fist, a very violent Blow upon the right Temple, which threw her into a Fit, and deprived her of her Senses (which Fits, she, this Informant, saith she is accustomed and subject to, upon being frighted, and that they often continue for six or seven Hours. . .)"

"Stay, stay, sir," I implored, "for here is such a foyson of this Informant, and the said Informanat, as carries me back to the Court of Session, whence I am newly a truant; so pray, sir, give me the straight of the story without circumlocution."

"Well, then, sir: Bet Canning told a horrid tale,

how these pandours in bob-wigs snatched her up by Bedlam Gate, and carried her off in her fit. They carried her off to a bawdy-house in the suburbs, said Bet; and there an old woman took her by the hand, and My dear, says she, will you go our way? For if you do, you shall have fine clothes. No, says Bet. Straightway the old woman takes up a carving-knife, and cuts the lace of the girl's stays, which the men in bob-wigs had overlooked, and takes them from her. Then she feels of the girl's petticoats. These are of no use, says she, I'll give you them. With that she gives the girl a great slap in the chops, and turns her up a pair of stairs, half-naked as she was, into a kind of loft or shuffleboard room. There, said Betty, she found some old mouldy bread and a broken jug full of water; but for which, and a penny minced pye which she happened to have by her, she had starved to death. For eight-and-twenty days no soul came nigh her. On the five-and-twentieth day the bread was all gone. On the eight-and-twentieth day she broke out at the window and ran away home."

"Sure, sir," I cried, "these were no Christians, but heathen Turks, so to misuse a poor innocent girl!"

"Yet you will allow, sir, that 'tis an excess of Christianity, thus to suffer for eight-and-twenty days an unnecessary martyrdom; for she who can break out at a window on the eight-and-twentieth day of fasting, might have done so with less fatigue on the first."

"Heathen Turks," I reiterated hotly, "and I

heartily wish they may have been laid by the heels."

"As to Turks, Bozzy, you are not so far out; and as to laying by the heels, they were so. And a precious crew they proved to be, being the old bawd, Susannah Wells by name, and a parcel of gipsies, her lodgers. They carried the girl to the suburbs to identify the people and the place. This is the house, says Bet; this is the shuffleboard room; and these are the miscreants, says she, pointing at the gipsies. It was the old gipsy woman cut my stays; and I think, says she, I *think* the gipsy man her son was one of the men in bob-wigs; while as to the two gipsy wenches her daughters, though they laughed at me they did nothing to me. As to the old bawd, I don't know that ever I saw her in my life before."

"I hope," cried I, "that the whole precious crew have long since had their just deserts."

"No, sir," replied my friend coolly, " 'tis true, the world was once of your mind; Wells was branded in the hand, and the old gipsy woman was to hang for the stays. But the old woman found friends, who have so managed, that she had the King's pardon, and placed the girl in the dock in her stead."

"Upon what charge?" I cried.

"Upon a charge of perjury."

"Monstrous!" I exclaimed angrily. "How mean you, friends? The publican of some ale-house under a hedge?"

"No, sir," replied Dr. Johnson. "I will name but one: the Lord Mayor of London."

I gaped.

"You have wished to see the sights of London," remarked my friend. "Here is one you are not to pass by. The girl takes her trial today."

Now it was clear why my friend had caused me to hear the girl's story. The curtain was about to rise on a new act of the drama.

"Will you come, sir?"

"No, sir. I am too old and too thick in the middle to batter my way into the press at the Old Bailey."

I was young and spry. I clapped on my three-cornered hat and made off down Fleet Street to the Sessions House in the ancient street known as the Old Bailey.

Before I had turned the corner a muttering sound told me of the crowd that was milling uneasily in the paved court-yard. I was not to be daunted. I butted and pushed my way until I stood, half-suffocated, under the balcony and close by the dock.

On the long bench at the front sat the Justices of Oyer and Terminer, the lawyers in robes, the aldermen with their chains of office about their necks. On the floor before them a spry man with his bag-wig pushed back was talking in brisk tenor tones. But I had no eyes for them.

.   On the raised platform of the dock, clinging to the rail that fenced it, stood the girl. She was a stocky chit, no higher than five feet, drest in a clean linnen gown. She wore buckled shoes and a decent lawn kerchief, and her plain cap was fastened under her chin. The light fell on her pink, expressionless face. The spry lawyer was describing her in unflattering terms as a liar for profit; but the large blue eyes never flickered. Elizabeth Canning looked at him as if he weren't there at all.

Then her eyes shifted, and I followed her gaze. Seated to one side, in a large armed chair, sat the most hideous old hag I had ever had the misfortune to see. She was bent, and tremulous, and swarthy. Swathing clouts half-hid a face like a night-mare. She had a great frog's mouth smeared all over the lower half of her face. Her chin was aflame with the purple scars of an old disease, and her swarthy hooked nose jutted over all. This was Mary Squires, the gipsy beldame. She was attended by a sparkling dark girl and a trim-built young gipsy man.

I could not read the stolid girl's expression, as she looked at her enemy. It held neither indignation nor remorse, but something more like puzzlement.

For ten mortal hours I stood on my feet as the gipsy's witnesses followed one another on the stand.

"How is it with Canning?" asked Dr. Johnson as I supped with him. "Is she cast?"

"No, sir," I replied. "There are prosecution witnesses still to come, spare the defence; for length this trial bids fair to make history."

"Pray, how will it go?"

"Sir," I replied, "ill, I fear. Here have been forty witnesses come up from Dorset to swear an alibi for yonder gipsy hag. She was strolling, they will stand to it, through the Dorset market-towns peddling such smuggled goods as she might come by in the sea-ports. Here has been a most respectable witness, an exciseman, who will swear it, that they lay in the excise office at Abbotsbury on the very night. Here have been landlords of inns from Abbotsbury to London to trace them on their way, bar only a four-days' journey from Coombe to Basingstoke. They came to Enfield full three weeks after Canning absconded. How 'tis managed I know not, but the girl is devoted to doom."

A knocking interrupted my discourse. The knocker proved to be a heavy-set red-faced man. He was accompanied by a younger man, a spindle-shanked sandy fellow with a long nose. Between them they supported a weeping woman. The woman was fortyish, and ample to overflowing.

The sandy young man burst immediately into speech.

"Robert Scarrat, hartshorn-rasper, at your service, sir, which I rasps hartshorn on a piece basis for Mrs. Waller of Old 'Change, and her son is tenant to Mrs. Canning here."

The weeping woman snuffled and confirmed the hartshorn-rasper with a nod.

"This here," the nervous strident tones hurried on, "is by name John Wintlebury, as is landlord of the Weavers' Arms, and Bet Canning was a servant in his house."

" 'Tis a good wench," rumbled the publican.

"Nevertheless they have contrived her ruin among them," cried the woman, "and will transport

her to the plantations—unless you, sir, would undertake to clear up the matter."

"You must tell me," replied my friend, "what
they are saying about her."

" 'Tis never true that I hid her for my gain," cried
out the weeping mother, smearing her bleared eyes
with a thick finger, "for I never had rest, day nor
night, for wondering where she was. Mostly I
thought her dead in Houndsditch, sir, or catched up
by some rakish young fellow. I had dreams and
wandering thoughts, and I prayed day and night to
have a vision of her. But the cunning man said—"

"The cunning man?"

"A mere piece of woman's folly, sir," muttered
the innkeeper, but Mrs. Canning paid him no mind.

"The cunning man in the Old Bailey. I went to
him to have news of her, he had a black wig over his
face."

"What said he?"

"Not a word, sir, only wrote, scribble, scribble,
scribble along. He said, an old black woman had my
daughter, and she would return soon."

"Ay," chimed in the hartshorn-rasper, his prominent hazel eyes rolling with superstitious awe, "is't
not strange, sir?"

Mrs. Canning shuddered, and sobbed harder than
ever. The landlord laid his hand on the woman's
arm.

"Be easy, ma'am," he said gently, "for we know
Bet's a good girl, and Dr. Johnson will soon make the

matter clear. No need to take the hystericks over it."

The woman moaned. Scarrat took up the tale.

"Nor 'tis not true," he went on, "that I went off with the girl for my pleasure, for she was unknown to me."

"Ay," seconded the landlord, "for all the time she lived in my house, she was modest and shy, and would scarce so much as go to the door to speak to a man; and though Mr. Scarrat frequented the house, they never exchanged a word."

"And," cried the spindly man, growing hot, "as to my forging this tale, out of revenge against the bawd, 'tis false as Hell, though indeed I owe the creature no kindness."

"A notorious woman," said Wintlebury, "I knew of her infamous brothel when I lived and courted in Hertford."

"Oh, pray, pray, Dr. Johnson," sobbed out the weeping mother, "will not you help us?"

"Do, sir," I seconded. "Could you but see the vile face of the gipsy hag, you would rush to the girl's defence."

"As to faces," replied my friend, "there's no art to find in them the mind's construction; and as to helping, if I must come down to the Old Bailey, 'twill not do."

The fat woman gave a howl and fell to the floor in a paroxysm. There was instant confusion. The fat friend and the thin one fell to slapping her wrists, while I applied under her snubby nose the hartshorn-bottle which was perhaps the fruit of Mr. Scarrat's endeavours.

When she had gasped and sat up, I turned to my kindly friend.

"Pray give your assistance," I begged. "I will be your deputy to the Old Bailey."

My friend accepted of my offer, and the friends of Canning departed in better cheer.

Only the fame of my companion gained us access to the gipsy. She sat in the best room of the White Horse, in the Haymarket, and regarded us sardonically with black, beady eyes. She was surrounded by a court of Dorsetshire fishermen, King's landwaiters, and gipsies in leather breeches. Her pretty daughter sat hand in hand with a tall man in fustian; I recognized with a start one of the principal witnesses for the prosecution, a cordwainer of Dorset. A black-browed little raisin of a man turned out to be the girl's uncle, Samuel Squires, a landwaiter of the customs right here in London and a gipsy of considerable influence.

Dr. Johnson ran a lowering eye over the motley crew; the men of the customs particularly took his eye. Then he waved them all away, and to my relief they went.

"Now, ma'am," says Dr. Johnson, "out with it. There's more in this than meets the eye."

The beady eyes measured him.

"I will confess," said the rusty voice.

I thrilled to my toes. The girl was saved!

"I'll confess. Though I have passed myself for a strolling pedlar, I am in reality—"

Dr. Johnson leaned forward.

"I am in reality—a *witch*. I can be present at *two* places at one time," whispered the old beldame with hoarse and ostentatious caution, "and though all these people saw me in Dorset, I neverthreless carried Canning to Enfield on my *broom-stick*—"

Dr. Johnson cut short her triumphant cackle by rising to his feet.

"Have a care, ma'am," he said angrily, "I am not to be trifled with."

The old hag leaned back and laughed in his face.

"I know you are no witch," my friend went on grimly, "but I will tell you what you are."

He spoke three words in her ear. Her face changed. She looked at him with more respect.

"Ah," she said, "I see you are in the councils of the great."

"I can see a church by daylight," replied Johnson as we withdrew.

I made off, being engaged to dine with some ladies in St. James's, but Dr. Johnson turned into the tap-room and lingered.

"Alack, Mr. Boswell," he told me when again we met. "Alas for Bet Canning, the rusticks are honest. I had their story over a can of ale, and with such a wealth of detail as can scarce be forgery. The honest cordwainer loves the gipsy wench; he dallied eight days in their company at Abbotsbury, and when they departed he followed them on the road. There are landlords to swear to them all, and the things they saw and the meals they ate. So rich is the tale, it must be more than mendacious invention."

"Yet who pays," I cried, "who pays the scot of the poor gipsy pedlar and her forty witnesses at the White Horse in the Haymarket? Who keeps them in victuals and gin?"

"My Lord Mayor, 'tis said," replied my companion. "But come, Mr. Boswell, let me know your mind: shall we push forward and uncover the truth, wherever it lies? Or shall we leave Bet Canning to her luck with the jury?"

"Let us wait," I replied uneasily, "and see."

I filled the days of waiting in the court-room of the Old Bailey, where each day the girl sat in the dock with her wrists crossed before her, and looked on without expression while witnesses called her liar or martyr.

"How goes the trial, Bozzy?" demanded my friend as I returned bedraggled from another day's session.

"Ill, for the girl, ill," I replied dejectedly. "You may know how ill, when I tell you that the Lord Mayor was pelted by the resentful Canningite rabble as he came away from the Sessions-house. The girl has been made to appear a liar. Before the sitting Aldermen, so he has sworn, she described her prison to be little, square, and dark. Then they took her to Enfield; when it appeared that the room she swore to was long and light, with many other contradictions. I know not what to think.''

A starved girl, after long imprisonment, may surely exhibit some confusion,'' suggested Dr. Johnson thoughtfully.

"There is more," I replied. "From Enfield came many witnesses, who swore that they visited her supposed prison during that month, and saw there no such person as Elizabeth Canning."

"What said the girl to this?"

"Never a word, save once. 'Twas a son of Wells's testified, he stepped into the shuffleboard room to lay by his tools, for he is a carpenter, and there was no soul there save the labouring man that lodged there. Bet Canning leaned forward, and scanned him closely. She frowned, and looked him up and down. *I never saw him before, as I know of,* says she."

"Why did she so?"

"Who can tell? 'Tis a strange wench. Just so, by the evidence, did she comport herself when they took her to Enfield: would not be sure of the gipsy man, could not be sure she had ever seen Wells. Only the gipsy woman she swore to without hesitation. They report strange things of the girl, too, in Wells's loft. *Do you remember that six-foot nest of drawers?* says they. *I never saw it before,* says Miss. *Do you remember the hay and the saddles stored up here?* says they. She scratches her head. *I will not swear,* says she, *but there is more hay. As to the saddles, I remember one only. But there was a grate,* says she. *O no,* says they, *look for yourself. There's no grate and never has been: look at the cobwebs. There was a grate, says she, and from it I took the rags I wore when I fled. There was never a grate, says they."*

"Is it so!" cried my venerable friend. "Here is no liar, but one trying to speak the truth. Bozzy, we must save this girl!"

I stared. The evidence, that had shaken my faith in the girl, had spoken quite otherwise to him. It had spoken with such clear moral force and conviction that it stirred his great bulk, and brought it next morning into the court-room of the Old Bailey.

He cleared his way through the press like a bailiff, with jerks of his sturdy oak staff. We were in time to hear the defence begin. The crowd murmured in sympathy as Bet's sad story was repeated by her friends as they had heard it from her on that Monday in January. All her natural functions were suspended, related the apothecary in sepulchral tones, the whole time of her imprisonment; she was very faint and weak, and the black-and-blue marks never went off for a month afterwards. My venerable friend shook his head from side to side, and clicked his tongue.

Burning glances of sympathy were levelled at the abused girl where she sat impassive in the dock as the story was told. They changed to looks of triumph as the defence brought aces out of their sleeves—a witness who had seen the girl led past his turnpike, in tears, by a pair of ruffians; three persons who had seen the bedraggled creature returning in the misty evening.

Dr. Johnson, seated on a bench with his chin on his staff, frowned and shook his head.

"How can this help?" he muttered. "The girl swore she was dragged off in a fit. Now we find she walked by the turnpike. Where is truth to be found?"

The defence rested.

It was three o'clock the next morning when I knocked up my friend.

"The girl is cast!" I told him. "She will be transported."

"Cast!" exclaimed my friend. "What this girl has been, I know not; but she is no perjurer."

A double knock announced a later walker than I. Again it was John Wintlebury and Robert Scarrat.

"You must help us!" cried the hartshorn-rasper. "Can you give us no hope?"

"Only this, that the girl is innocent," replied my friend. "I will do what I can. Where is the girl?"

"Alack," exclaimed the volatile Scarrat, "in Newgate."

"Then we must have her out."

That was easier said than done, but Johnson managed it. Scarrat carried the request. Meanwhile, off went the black boy Francis to the White Horse. He came back with a note:

"She says she will come, if only to laugh.
                                        Ma: Squires"

The old gipsy woman herself was not far behind. Next to arrive was Mother Wells. She came supported by the carpenter son. My friend received his curious callers with solemn dignity, and offered them cakes and port. The wrinkled old bawd guzzled hers with coarse greed.

It was still dark night when a sedan-chair turned into Johnson's Court. It was attended by two turnkeys and followed by our friends, once again supporting between them the highstrung matron. All three tenderly extracted from the chair the stocky person of Elizabeth Canning, and so she was assisted up the stair.

Dr. Johnson took her hand.

"Do not be afraid, my dear."

"I am not afraid," said Bet Canning.

She looked levelly at the hideous old gipsy hag, then at the bawd. The latter wiped a drool of port off her chin. Dr. Johnson handed the girl to a chair, her friends found places, and a hush fell as everyone in the room looked toward my learned friend.

"My dear," said Dr. Johnson, addressing himself to the girl, "there are those who think you are lying. I do not think you are lying."

"Thank you, sir."

The gipsy beldame, a mere huddle of rags except for her bright black eyes, snorted.

"But, my dear," my friend continued quietly, "there is much that is dark, much that you have not been able to tell us."

"I have told," said Bet Canning clearly, "all that I know."

"We must look further, then. There is one in this cause," said Dr. Johnson, "who seemed a knowledgeable man."

I leaned forward.

"Who?"

"The cunning man," replied my learned friend solemnly. "He knew where Elizabeth was, and he wrote it down, scribble, scribble, scribble along. He was right. I would have consulted him myself, but he is not to be found. There is no conjurer in the Old Bailey."

"I saw him there myself," cried Mrs. Canning. "He had his wig over his face; and when he lighted up the candles, he frighted me, and I could not stay for more."

"Well, well, he is gone away from thence, he is no longer to be consulted. We must make do without him."

He produced a leather case, which being opened revealed a gleaming polished disc of some black substance.

"This," said Dr. Johnson solemnly, "is the famous Black Stone of Dr. Dee the alchemist. I had it of Mr. Walpole against this night's purpose. Into it," he lowered his sonorous voice another pitch, "the alchemist used to call his spirits, and they revealed the truth to him."

Nobody spoke.

Dr. Johnson extinguished the candles, all but one,

which gleamed fitfully on the table, accentuating rather than piercing the darkness. For a moment there was dead silence.

"Before the spirits speak," said Dr. Johnson, "has no one a word to tell us?"

I heard somebody gasp. The old gipsy was shaking and muttering to herself, it might have been a charm or an incantation. Mrs. Canning was crying again, in long shuddering gasps, and the hartshorn-rasper was twitching where he sat. Only the stolid inn-keeper and the cynical old bawd preserved an unbroken calm.

Elizabeth Canning's gaze caught and hung on the gleaming speculum. Her plain face was white as paper.

"Pray, my girl," said Dr. Johnson gently, "look into the magick stone of Dr. Dee, and tell us what you see."

"I see nothing," she faltered.

"You will see the truth," said my friend. "Look well, and tell us what you see."

The girl stared into the polished surface, scarcely seeming to breathe. Her eyes contracted to pinpoints. She sat rigid.

"It is the night of January I," breathed my friend in the silence. "Do you see Elizabeth Canning?"

"I see her."

The voice was tight and high, and seemed to come from a long way off.

"I see Elizabeth Canning. She is walking between two men, and weeping. It is a road, with water in it.

Now they turn into a house, there is an old woman there."

"Swarthy and black?"

"No, grey and wrinkled. She takes away her clothes, and puts her into a room."

"Without any furniture?"

"No," replied the trance-like voice. "No, it is the best bedroom. The door opens, and the man comes in. Now Elizabeth can see his face. It is he. It is the same man who wanted Elizabeth to do the bad thing, always and always he was at her elbow saying it to her, and she would not. Now he is here to do it, and Elizabeth cannot help herself."

In a violent shudder the dreaming voice died away. For a moment there was silence in the room.

"Here," muttered Wintlebury finally, "you must stop this, sir, you've bewitched the girl to her hurt. Who knows what she'll say?"

"She'll say the truth," said Dr. Johnson sharply. "Be silent, sir, and listen."

He spoke soothingly to the rigid girl.

"It is the eve of King Charles's Martyrdom. Do you see Elizabeth Canning?"

"I see her."

"Where is she?"

"She is in the loft. The wicked man has left her behind, they have taken away her clothes, she cannot eat for shame. Because she would not do the bad thing with other men, they have beaten her and thrust her into the loft. She wants to go home, but she does not know where home is. She has forgotten her name. She has forgotten everything. She is very wretched."

Again the level voice died away.

"And then?"

The polished disc gleamed in the candlelight.

"And then she hears her name spoken, and she knows it is hers. She looks down into the kitchen and sees the ugly-face gipsy. She is hungry and cold and afraid. The minced pye is still in the pocket of her torn petticoat; it is stale and dry, but she eats it. She takes an old rag from the fireplace to wrap herself in, and breaks out at the window, and runs away home."

"But the grate?" I struck in.

"A saw across the fireplace," said a quiet voice in my ear. It was the young carpenter. "My cross-cut saw."

"She runs away home. They ask where she has been for four weeks; but she has forgotten. Only it seems to her that she was somewhere hungry and cold, and she has been somehow harmed, the ugly-face woman must have done it, and her cloathes are gone; so she tells them as best she can what must have happened, and they believe her, and are very angry. Even the man who did the bad thing to her, he is angry too, and wants the gipsy hanged. Elizabeth has forgotten what he did to her; she thinks he is her friend."

"The man," Dr. Johnson leaned forward gently, "who was the man?"

"That's enough of this flummery," came an angry

voice. "Can't you see that the girl is mad?"

A rough hand struck aside the magick speculum of Dr. Dee. Elizabeth Canning looked up into an out-thrust face, somehow distorted in the flickering light of the candle from below, and recoiled with scream after scream of terror. Then the candle flame was struck out, and footsteps clattered on the stair.

"Let him go," said Dr. Johnson. "Mr. John Wintlebury is not the first to enforce his desires on a virtuous serving-wench, and I fear there's no law to touch him."

"I'll touch him," cried the hartshorn-rasper violently. "I'll—I'll rasp him!"

He held the shuddering girl tight against his shoulder. He touched her pale hair.

"She's not mad, sir?" he pleaded.

"Not the least in the world," replied my friend, "yet hers is a strange affliction. The learned call it the catalepsy. One so afflicted may preach, or prophesy, or fast without hunger, or cut his flesh with knives, and not feel it; or fall unconscious and lie as the dead; or believe the body's functions to be pretermitted; or they may upon great suffering or shame forget who they are, and wander homeless until they remember. It was Mr. John Wintlebury's good luck that the wronged girl forgot him and the wrong he did her, and even herself, for very shame."

"And my bad luck," croaked the gipsy crone, "for the story that came from her disturbed mind put me into jeopardy of my life."

"You were never in jeopardy, being what you are," returned Dr. Johnson.

"What are you?" I burst out uncontrollably.

"A customs spy," replied the old witch, "and a good one, young man. Who'd ever suspect the old gipsy beggar when she came nosing about the barns? I knew every smugglers' lay on that coast. O no, me Lord Treasurer wouldn't have let the old gipsy woman hang. 'Twas but a few nights lying hard in gaol; he could not move openly in the matter, for fear of betraying me and mine to the smugglers. In the end me Lord Mayor had his orders, and I was enlarged."

"And Mother Wells?" I touched flint and steel to the candle.

"It all happened," my friend replied, "of course, in her house of assignation; it was she who beat the girl when she would not go the way of the house."

I advanced the candle toward the old bawd's corner. The lees of her port were there in the glass, but the old woman was gone.

"Upon her," remarked Dr. Johnson, "justice has been done. You will remember that, although Mary Squires was pardoned, Susannah Wells has been branded on the hand for her part in the work."

Elizabeth Canning's sobs had died away, and she lay in a sleep like death against the hartshorn-rasper's shoulder.

"When she awakes," he asked, "will she remember?"

"I cannot say," replied my learned friend. "Perhaps she will remember everything. If not, you must tell her, gently, over and over, until the two times join into one in her mind and she no longer has those agonizing moments of trying to remember, like the time in the loft, or in the dock when she struggled to remember the young carpenter."

He pulled aside the heavy curtains and let in the dawn.

"Tomorrow," he said, "I will wait upon the Secretary of State."

The sun was up as the sleepy turnkeys rouzed to help lift the unconscious girl back into the sedanchair. My benevolent friend followed it with his eyes to the mouth of the court.

"The issue of this night's sitting," he remarked with a half-smile, "has exceeded expectation. I reasoned that someone close to the girl knew where she was, else why the cunning man with the muffled face, who must write his predictions? Clearly his face and his voice were known. I brought her friends together, and produced a conjuration of my own. I hoped that superstition would affright one of them, and even that the girl might take courage and 'see' in the speculum what perhaps she had been frighted from telling. I never guessed that so strange is the mind in a catalepsy that it will see truly, as it were in a sleep, what it has forgotten in waking."

[The disappearance of Elizabeth Canning from her aunt's house in London in 1753 was a nine-days' wonder which was not solved in her time. To make a story of it, I advanced the date to bring it under Boswell's eye, and supplied an invented solution which came to me one night in sleep. Working it up along those lines, I soon came to see that my subconscious had hit upon the actual and only possible solution of the bizarre affair. The whole story will be found in my *Elizabeth Is Missing* (New York: Alfred A. Knopf, Inc., 1945). There the curious reader may find how the matter actually came out (without the intervention of Dr. Johnson) and what kind of a happy ending Elizabeth Canning actually met with, and where.]

THE BLACKAMOOR UNCHAIN'D

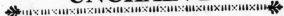

The Negro was chained to the mainmast, and the vessel was clearing for Jamaica. No better prospect appeared at journey's end for him than the slave block, the plantation, the cane-brake, and the lash.

What remedy?

But let us take things in order.

That my learned friend, Dr. Sam: Johnson, *detector* of crimes and righter of wrongs, was openly zealous in opposing the institution of human slavery, is well known.

"Here's to the next insurrection of the Negroes in the West Indies!"

Such was the toast with which, I am told, he once scandalized some very grave scholars at Oxford.

Insurrections there were in plenty among the black slaves on the plantations of Jamaica, and they were put down in torture and blood. Such episodes rouzed my moral friend's deepest indignation.

"Jamaica!—great wealth and dreadful wickedness—a den of tyrants!" I have heard him growl.

"It is impossible," he declared more coolly, "not to conceive that men in their original state were equal."

That he genuinely thought so, in spite of his spectacular attacks on frantick "levellers" like Mrs. Macaulay, was abundantly proved by the tenderness and respect he extended to his black servant, Frank Barber.

Frank came to him from that very "den of tyrants," Jamaica, brought thence in his boyhood as body-servant to a plantation owner. Left his freedom and a legacy in his owner's will, Frank came into Johnson's service before my time, in the year 1752, close upon Mrs. Johnson's lamented death; and Johnson's "boy" he had been ever since.

Tho' in this spring of 1772 he was thirty years of age or more, he still looked the youthful foot-boy, for he was of slender make and low stature, and his blue-black countenance never lost its look of innocence. He was narrow of shoulder and flank, and had a thin neck, spindle shanks, and long slim black hands faintly pink in the palm. His head was round and fuzzed with closecurled woolly hair. His thick lips pursed, his large black eyes shewed an ivory gleam as they moved. He spoke softly, with a lazy lilt, but correctly, for Dr. Johnson had seen him well schooled.

On 21 March, 1772, I—James Boswell, advocate, your most obedient—came once more from my dwelling in Edinburgh to visit my friends in London. Setting myself to rights, I hastened to wait upon my revered friend Dr. Sam: Johnson at his house in Johnson's Court.

Frank answered the door, trim in fustian breeches and striped waistcoat.

"You are welcome to London, Mr. Boswell. Dr. Johnson is with Miss Williams. This way, sir."

In the ground-floor apartment of Miss Williams, the blind poetess, I found Dr. Johnson by the teapot, and a storm brewing in it. While Frank procured and dressed the viands, Miss Williams presided over the household economy, and the pair, thus divided in authority, were often at odds. To-day, in her lady-like soft voice, she scolded Dr. Johnson about the alleged short-comings of his black attendant.

"So, Dr. Johnson," she uttered sarcastically, "there (pointing at Frank)—there stands your 'scholar,' your 'philospher'—"

Frank beat a hasty retreat.

"—upon educating whom you have spent so many hundreds of pounds! And how are you repaid? Waste! Where's the rest of the pork and pease? Where's yesterday's loaf? Who drank the milk jug empty?"

"Perhaps the *Pook*, who sweeps the hearth by night, and drinks out the milk in payment," suggested my friend, rallying her mildly. "We had such beneficent *Brownies* about the kitchen, Mr. Boswell, when I was a child in Lichfield."

"I doubt it not," returned Miss Williams smartly, she being Welsh and of a credulous turn, "and that's another thing. Your house is haunted, sir, there's something walks in the attick."

"Frank by name, I suppose, since he is bedded there."

"It has walked while Frank was before me."

"It walks in the attick and eats the cold victuals," I summed up. "Here's a *mystery* for you, sir."

" 'Tis soon solved. Follow me, Mr. Boswell, to the attick."

"Where you'll find, I warrant you, that Frank has been up to mischief," Miss Williams tossed after us.

There was no appearance of mischief about the woebegone figure on the bed in the attick. A quilt was pulled about the narrow shoulders, the round woolly head was turned to the wall.

"What, Frank lad, art ill, boy?" enquired Dr. Johnson with concern.

The blue-black countenance turned to us. Simultaneously there was a clatter on the stair, and Frank Barber came into the room.

We stared. The unknown blackamoor was thin and gaunt, and his kinky head was bandaged. He turned dark eyes upon us, and said nothing.

"So here's our ghost," observed Dr. Johnson.

"And our *Brownie* too," I added, "that eats up the victuals."

"I found him starving in the street," burst out Frank. "Sure, sir, you'd never grudge him a bite and a sup?"

"Why, boy, you know I would not," rejoined Johnson gravely, "so why this secrecy?"

"I promised it him, sir. He's an escaped slave, and fears recapture."

"A slave? In London?" I interjected.

"Why, then," replied Dr. Johnson, "he's but one of many. The West Indians bring them hither, as Frank was brought. Well, my lad, account for yourself. Who's your master?"

"Stand up!" admonished Frank anxiously, "and make a reverence to the gentleman."

The fellow came slowly to his feet. Like Frank, he was low of stature and slender of build, with lank shanks and long slim hands, and his dusky visage bore a look both innocent and proud. He wore an old shirt of Frank's and nothing else. He executed a kind of awkward salaam, at which Frank nodded approval, and spoke in a musical drawl.

"Cap'n Standart, Sallee Plantation, Jamaica. Cap'n beat me—"

"He beat him without provocation," put in Frank, "under drink taken, and broke his head, as you see." The fellow nodded and touched his bandage. "What could he do but run, and what could I do but succour him?"

"What's your name, boy?" asked my friend gently.

"Quashie, marsa."

"He may stay?" enquired Frank anxiously.

"Quashie may stay, and share your couch and your victuals."

To my surprise, Quashie, beaming, expressed his satisfaction in song:

"Calipash! Calipee!" his ditty ran, in a sweet plaintive voice:

>   "Calipash! Calipee!
>   "O how happy us all be!"

He even essayed a little dance step on his long slim black feet.

"No more o' that, Quashie!" said Frank sharply, scandalized; "make your reverence and retire."

"Well, be easy, Quashie," smiled Dr. Johnson, "Frank shall take care of you till we see what must be done with you."

"Not go back to Cap'n!" cried Quashie in alarm. "Never!"

"I hope not, Quashie. But 'tis a touchy affair, and must be thought on. Come, Mr. Boswell."

He led the way down the stair, shaking his head.

"What will become of poor Quashie, I know not."

"Surely," I said, "no man can hold a slave in England?"

"That's to be seen," replied my friend. "The matter is *sub judice* before Lord Chief Justice Mansfield. There's a cause before him between an escaped slave, Somerset by name, and his former master. Till 'tis settled. Quashie must keep close."

"What hinders the settling?"

"There are fourteen thousand such slaves in England. My Lord Mansfield shrinks from freeing them all at once with his single word. He'd like to find an excuse, as he has done before, lack of documents or so, to set this particular slave free and spare the general judgment. But this time he's caught a

Tartar. Somerset won't have it, nor will his sponsor, the noted crusader against slavery, Mr. Granville Sharp. Nor, for his part, will the master neither.

"But Lord Mansfield procrastinates, and thus the fate of Quashie hangs in the balance, and that of fourteen thousand like him. Meanwhile the boy is Captain Standart's property, and may be shipped out for Jamaica, there to be worked, lashed, even killed, at pleasure. We must keep him under cover."

That was easier said than done. If one black boy in Johnson's Court was a curiosity, two were a nine days' wonder. Soon we had a visitation.

The visitant was a thin, sallow, upright personage in a red coat. He presented himself in the one-pair-of-stairs sitting room, bowed stiffly, curtly uttered his name—"Captain Standart, to command—" and came straight to the point:

"It comes to my ears, sir, that you are detaining my neger slave Quashie, and I require you'll hand him over instanter."

Standing four-square before the fire-place in his old rusty brown broadcloth, Dr. Johnson put up his well-marked brows.

"Require?"

"Yes, sir, require. I demand my property."

"Your property? That's to be seen."

"Aye, sir, my property, to the value of fifty pounds, which he'll fetch on the slave black in Jamaica."

"You must catch him first," smiled Johnson.

"I'll catch him, never fear," snarled Captain

Standart, "and I'll have the law on *you* for a thief."

"As to that, the law shall decide."

But the Captain was breathing fire and alcohol. He had come to bully his antagonist, and when one threat failed to move my intrepid friend, he was ready with another.

"D-mn the law!" he exclaimed. "You shall answer to me in person."

"Why, so I do, I answer, do your worst."

"You shall answer in the field."

"How, a duello!" I exclaimed, half aghast, half excited.

"If old square-toes don't fear me," sneered the Captain uncivilly.

"I hold the duello in abhorrence," said my moral friend calmly, "yet I don't fear you. I'll meet you, sir, at the time and place, and with the weapons of my choice, as is the right of the challenged."

"Then chuse," snapped the soldier.

"I chuse *here* and *now,* and for weapons—here are weapons to hand (indicating the fire-irons). You may take the poker, and I'll make shift with the tongs."

So saying, he seized them up and made them to snap a scant inch from the startled slave-owner's nose.

"Unheard of!" ejaculated the Captain, backing off.

"You have no taste for my weapons? Nor I for yours. I'll not run you through or shoot you down, sir, for Scripture bids us do no murder; but I'll wring your nose if I can come at it," cried the burly philosopher, snapping the tongs wildly, "so *en garde*!"

"The man is mad!" cried the Jamaican, dodging in alarm. He gained the door, flung it open, and was gone. We heard his boots clatter on the stair, and Dr. Johnson's Olympian laughter followed him.

"A pretty brute to *own* a man," he observed, sobering. "We must keep Quashie out of his hands."

Again time passed. Quashie mended and grew strong. We would hear his delighted chuckle below stairs, or his mellow voice singing strange little melodies by the kitchen fire. He had a ditty for every contingency. "Rain crowd fly away" greeted the downpour. "Stranger come riding" announced the caller. "Calipash! Calipee!" did for grace before meat. This mysterious incantation, I learned, called upon the Jamaicans' favorite comestible, green turtle.

No such regale of Aldermen adorned Dr. Johnson's table; but Quashie was equally happy with the pork and pease, and gobbled it down. This pained Frank, who strove earnestly to improve his protégé's demeanour; but cheerfulness was always breaking in. Miss Williams delighted to hear Quashie sing, and the pair quietly made up an alliance against Frank's authority, at which Dr. Johnson smiled indulgently. He had come to repose confidence in Quashie's ministrations, approved his progress under Frank's tutelage, and meditated sending him, too, to be schooled in the country. But fate interposed.

One bright May morning, when we returned from breakfasting abroad, Quashie was gone.

"Where is Quashie?" repeated Miss Williams fretfully. "Why do you ask, sir, when you sent for him yourself, to fetch your prayer book to the Mitre?"

"My *prayer book?* What would I be about, with a prayer book at a tavern?"

"Nay, sir, who knows your whim? Frank was gone for provisions, and Quashie found the book where it lies on your bureau, and ran off with it."

"He ran, I fear, straight into the hands of Captain Standart, who has thus tricked us all."

"What's to be done?" I cried.

"Nay, I know not. He may be any where, and meeting any fate, even death itself."

"Come, sir," I urged, making for the street door, "we cannot sit idle."

" 'Twill not help to run about at random. No, sir, we must have intelligence to proceed upon."

As we stood at the door, wondering thus which way to turn, a hackney coach clattered into the court, and pulled up before us.

"One of you Sam: Johnson?" demanded the coachman hoarsely.

"I am Sam: Johnson."

The coachman dropped the reins. His nag drooped in an attitude of repose, and the fellow descended. He smelled of gin and horse.

"This is your prayer book?"

He shewed the neat script on the fly leaf: *Sam: Johnson, Johnson's Court.*

I could sense my friend's excitment, but he answered calmly enough:

"It is mine. How did you come by it?"

"Worth a little something, an't it?" demanded the coachman.

"Perhaps; and more, if you tell me where you got it."

"I didn't steal it," said the fellow truculently.

"Of course not. Where did you find it, then? For a shilling (producing one)."

"Two," said the Jehu instantly.

For answer I pulled a shilling from my pocket and held it up next to Johnson's. The coachman looked from shilling to shilling, seemed minded to have more, and then shrugged.

"At the West India docks."

"At the docks! Does a ship lie there?"

"Yes, sir, the *Guinea Gold* is laden; she'll sail for Jamaica with the morning tide."

"Bravo, Quashie!" cried Dr. Johnson. "By dropping the book, he has contrived to send us a message. You, friend, is your coach for hire?"

"What else?"

"Then here's your two shillings, and a third for earnest. You shall be ours for the day."

"Ben Handey's at your sarvice, gentlemen both."

I was for speeding straight to the docks. But the first errand, it seemed, was to the milliner, whither

Frank was sent with a billet, and whence he returned with a large band-box. Meanwhile, Dr. Johnson donned his best array, full-skirted purple camlet coat and large bushy grizzled wig of state.

Soon our little entourage was ready to take coach. Dr. Johnson carried his stout oak stick. Frank Barber attended us. At him I stared. He was tricked out like a courtesan's monkey, in a brocaded caftan—somewhat the worse for wear—and a large swathed turban with fringes enclosed his inky countenance.

"Well, Dr. Johnson," I remarked, "I never thought to see you attended by such a gaudy page."

"Among West Indian nabobs," replied my friend, "it behooves us to cut a figure. Frank, have you the gallipot?"

"Yes, sir (shewing such a small pot as ladies use for pomatum)."

"Have you the tools?"

"In my waistcoat pockets, sir."

"Then let us go. Drive on, Handey."

A motley posse, we rattled towards the docks. I marvelled how we were to gain access to the ship; but I was soon instructed.

We scented the vessel before we saw it.

"Phew," I ejaculated, "what cargo does she carry, that stinks so perniciously?"

"Don't you know, sir? She's a slaver. 'Tis human cargo that smells so high. Pah!" Ben Handey spat emphatically. "Guinea gold, that's slaves, sir. The stench of 'em can't be quelled. She beats about the triangle—gauds and cloth out to the Guinea coast, there to trade for slaves, and carry them by the middle passage for sale in Jamaica, and so home laden with rum, sugar, and tobacco. 'Tis very profitable."

" 'Tis infamous," growled Dr. Johnson. "But what does she in London port? That's a Liverpool trade."

"Nay, I know not, but there she lies."

The *Guinea Gold* was a dirty-looking vessel of small tonnage, with dingy sails furled, linked to the dock by a plank walk. From the deck a burly person in authority looked across. Dr. Johnson measured him, and coolly mounted.

"Captain—?"

"Westover, what then?"

"From the City Wharfinger," I recited my lesson. I knew not whether there was such an official, but as it fell out, Captain Westover, unused to London port, knew no more than I; and my words were backed by a most impressive document of Johnson's concocting, gaudily sealed in red. The Captain frowned at it myopically.

"As Inspector of Wharves," said I glibly, "I am directed to view your ship before she sails; and my friend comes with me, Colonel Johnson, a wealthy nabob of Barbadoes, who having money to put out, desires to see how the slave trade goes on."

"Scurvily," grumbled the Captain; "but view what you will. Mr. MacNeill!"

MacNeill proved to be the ship's supercargo, a sandy little tight-mouthed person who led us about in silence. We walked the deck, where sailor-men in loose pantaloons and tarry pigtails busied themselves mysteriously with coils of rope. They stared curiously at Frank's gauds, but said nothing. I drew from my pocket the tablets I invariably carry about me (to record my friend's memorable discourses) and officiously made notes. Quashie, the real object of our search, was nowhere to be seen.

From the deck we descended the stair to the chart room and the officers' quarters. All was narrow and dark and empty, but shipshape and ready to clear. No Quashie.

We passed forward to the forecastle, where dwelt the crew. We saw their few hammocks and sleeping gear trussed up out of the way against the wooden side. Well forward, a thin sailor in greasy slops scoured a pot. He gave us a surly look. No Quashie.

"So, sir," said MacNeill, "you've seen how we live. Will it please you go up?"

"No, sir," said Johnson, "we'll go down."

"As you will," shrugged MacNeill. "The hold is in order, but I fear it won't please you."

The stench from the open hatch was already turning our stomachs, but we descended the narrow ladder, and stood in the darkness of the hold. I felt Frank shudder. As our eyes adjusted, we saw that the airless space, barely six feet high, was ringed round about by a double shelf, too low for a man to sit erect. MacNeill became voluble.

"On these shelves," said he, "we may transport

two or three hundred blacks from Guinea to Jamaica, chained two and two—"

The chains were visible, stapled to the wall.

"And on the voyage out to Guinea, as you see, the shelves serve for the trinkets and trade goods."

Indeed the surfaces were crammed with boxes and bales. Loading was done, and the ship was ready to sail.

"And what's this ironmongery?" With his oak stick, Dr. Johnson poked at a tangle of implements in a recess.

"Why, sir, to control the negers."

With a shudder I made out the sinister shape of a cat-o'-nine-tails with barbed lashes, spiked collars, leg-irons, and manacles. My gorge rose.

"Well thought on," said Johnson coolly; "and what's backwards of the hatch?"

"More shelves, sir; and there, of course, the mainmast is stepped."

We made it out by the faint light from the hatch over head, a great oak tree trunk, affixed to the ship's spine; and against it, as if embracing it, sat poor Quashie. His slim wrists were encircled with iron bracelets, rivetted on, and a chain round the mast held him fast, so that he could sit or stand against it, but not turn away. He had no song now. He rolled his eyes upon us in silent despair.

"What's to do here?" asked Johnson, still maintaining his character of a stranger from Barbadoes.

"'Tis a runaway slave, sir, consigned to Jamaica to

be sold. They'll teach him better there, I warrant you," said MacNeill with satisfaction.

"And a good thing too," Dr. Johnson seconded the sentiment. "You, Frank, you scoundrel, look on him and be warned," he added with affected menace.

"Yes, marsa," said Frank.

"Well, let us go. Pray, Mr. MacNeill, go you before. You, Mister Wharfinger (politely naming me by my supposed function), shall boost from behind, and so I'll get myself up this precipice."

MacNeill shewed his agility by scampering up. Dr. Johnson put one foot to the ladder, and paused. His oak stick had vanished, and must be found. Frank and I were put to the search:

"Go you abaft the mainmast, Frank, and you, Mister Wharfinger, forward. And, Bozzy (calling after me), turn over the ironmongery."

Inwardly shrinking, I did so, setting up a prolonged clangour and clatter, before the lost object finally came to light by the ladder foot. Satisfied, my friend ascended another rung of the ladder, and again paused. This time the delay was caused by a slightly loose shoe buckle, which must be (with much difficulty and a handy scrap of packthread) secured, lest the wearer trip in ascending.

"Well, sir, what's the matter?" called MacNeill impatiently.

"Nothing, sir, all's put to rights. Here we come. Frank! Where's that rascal?"

"Here, marsa." Caftan and turban appeared beside us.

"Up we go! Boost, Frank! And you, Mister Wharfinger, pray pass up my stick and follow on."

I followed on. When I came up out of the noisome hold, I saw the departing flick of a brocade hem at the officers' stair head, and heard my friend's sonorous voice saying:

"Make haste, Frank! You must take coach and hurry to Johnson's Court with a billet."

At the stair foot, MacNeill stood gazing upward and scratching his ear. I tapped his shoulder and mumbled something about his papers. In his musty lair next the chart room, he placed them before me. After solemn scrutiny, I pronounced them in order, as indeed they were for aught I knew. Gratified, the supercargo pressed upon me some specimens of the ship's lading: sundry gaudy scraps of coarse cloth, with a handful of brummagem glass beads. I uttered profuse thanks, and took elaborate leave of him.

When I issued at last into the blessed clean air of the deck, Dr. Johnson's servitor had a written billet clutched in his greasy black hand, and was crossing the plank to the wharf, the while his master called after him:

"And hark'ee, Frank, bid the coachman make haste in returning."

An emphatick nod shook the turban fringes, and Ben Handey's coach jiggled them from our sight.

"All done?" rasped Captain Westover behind me.

"The report must be writ on the spot," cut in Dr. Johnson. "Be about it, Mister Wharfinger. You've time till Frank returns with an answer."

"An answer to what?" growled the Captain suspiciously.

"To my billet, sir," replied my friend blandly. "Now as to the blacks aboard ship, sir, pray tell, how do you manage—?"

He drew the scowling fellow into private discourse by the rail. My ears cauught scraps of the slaver's profane complaints about the perversity of the blackamoors and the difficulties of the slave trade. Warned by a glance from Dr. Johnson, I perched on a coil of rope, drew forth my tablets, and fell to scribbling. Having nothing official to record, I began to narrate the affecting story of Quashie. How would it end?

I did not see Frank come aboard, but when our hackney coach was once more perceived upon the wharf, Dr. Johnson pronounced:

"Frank must be returned. Frank!" he bellowed. "Where's my lacquey? He needs a beating. *Frank*!"

At this moment, who should come striding up the gang-plank but—Captain Standart! At sight of us he started.

"What, old square-toes, what do you here? After Quashie, no doubt? Well, I have him safe, sir. He'll soon learn his lesson."

"No doubt, sir," said Dr. Johnson coldly. "I'll bid you good day, sir. *Frank*!"

Up from below came Frank, his brocades gleaming, his wooley head bare.

"Quashie!" cried Captain Standart, collaring him. " 'Tis my black (shaking him)! How have you got loose? And in these cloathes!"

"No, sir," said Frank smoothly, in his best schooled English, "I am not your black: I am Dr. Johnson's black, and I desire you'll not detain me."

"There's something deep here," muttered Standart, loosing him reluctantly, "and I'll get to the bottom of it."

"Do," said Johnson, "go as deep in iniquity as you please, but stand out of my way (gripping his oaken stick). You, Frank, you scoundrel, where's your headgear?"

"Alack, sir, blown overboard."

Dr. Johnson caught him a smart box o' the ear.

"Be off, you ideot!"

To my amazement, the lofty philosopher, brandishing his stick, cudgelled Frank before him down the plank onto the wharf, while the black protected his pate with his arms. Captain Westover by the rail roared with laughter as at a comedy, and Captain Standart snorted and turned on his heel.

"Make haste, Ben," said Dr. Johnson, "for Captain Standart has gone below; he'll explode any minute."

As the Jehu encouraged his tired nag to exertion, sure enough there was a roar from the ship, and as we clattered away, Captain Standart started to the rail, his saturnine visage purple, and shook his fist after us.

BEN HANDEY: What ails the fellow?

JOHNSON (smiling): He has discovered the disappearance of Quashie.

BOSWELL: But what of the chain and manacles?

JOHNSON: 'Twas Frank that managed it. The hog's lard did it, boy?

FRANK: Yes, sir. The bracelets were meant for sailors' fists, not hands like ours (holding up a slim paw), and being well greased with hog's lard, such a hand could slip through. To my relief; for hammer and chisel, tho' I carried them about me, could not but prove noisier even than Mr. Boswell stirring up the ironmongery. Well, we got the fetters off, and caftan and turban on, while you, sirs, raised a dust at the ladder foot; and so Quashie passed for me long enough to slip away.

BOSWELL: What would you have done, Dr. Johnson, had the supercargo, becoming suspicious, descended the ladder again to oversee our proceedings?

JOHNSON: First tripping up his heels with my staff, sir, I should have then encumbered him with help, long enough for Quashie in Frank's caftan to make the best of his way up the ladder.

BOSWELL: Caftan? What then does Frank wear?

FRANK: A man may wear two caftans, one above the other.

BOSWELL (enlightened): But not two turbans.

"So the turban must seem lost," smiled Dr.

Johnson. "Sorry I am, Frank, that I had to beat you for it."

"More convincingly," rejoined Frank, "than painfully."

"It gave us a spectacular scene to exit by," observed Dr. Johnson, "and diverted the attention of the slavers momentarily from Quashie, long enough for us to elude them. We should not care to be in their hands now."

"So I was thinking, waiting in the hold for Quashie to get well away," said Frank. "I knew not but I should see Jamaica and slavery again."

"Well, boy, you have done nobly."

"Why Frank?" I burst out, aggrieved. "Why not me? Why was I excluded from the scheam?"

"Your face, my dear Bozzie," replied my friend, "is a window to your mind. Had you known 'twas Quashie between the turban fringes, your demeanor would have told the world of it."

"No, sir, you wrong me," said I quietly. "Could I fail to know one from 'tother, after weeks of seeing them together? Yet when you said 'Frank,' was I to cry 'Quashie'? To what end, think you did I clatter and clash the ironmongery so long and loud? To what end did I hold the supercargo in discourse while you sent off the black post-haste? No, sir, I have played my part, even uninstructed."

"Well done, Bozzy!" cried Dr. Johnson. "And prodigious well done, Frank! Between you, you have saved Quashie from slavery and oppression!"

Yet tho' Quashie had been rescued from the

vengeful Captain, in the Court of King's Bench before Lord Mansfield, Quashie's freedom, with Somerset's, still hung in the balance. I left England in late May. Not until June did I have a jubilant communication from Dr. Sam Johnson:

"You will rejoice to know, sir, that Somerset, and with him Quashie and all the rest, is finally free, by the noble efforts of Mr. Granville Sharp, and the judicial dictum of Lord Mansfield, who said:

"The air of England has long been too pure for a slave, and every man is free who breathes it!"

[Affairs like this one happened more than once in 18th Century London, and more than once the heroic abolitionist Granville Sharp (not, in reality, Dr. Sam: Johnson, strongly anti-slavery though he was) saved the abused Negro from a Jamaica-bound vessel, as we read in the *Memoirs* (Prince Hoare, *Memoirs of Granville Sharp, Esq.*, London: Henry Colburn, 1828, 2 vols.). Lord Mansfield's judgment in the Somerset case, which at last put a stop to such disgraceful episodes, is history. For a similar decision in the Scottish court, some time later, both Boswell and Johnson labored mightily.]

THE LOST HEIR
❀❀❀❀❀❀❀❀❀

"I implore you, Dr. Johnson, help a grieving mother to find her lost son!"

Thus impulsively spoke Paulette, Lady Claybourne, as she crossed the threshold at Johnson's Court. We saw a delicate small personage, past youth indeed, but slim and erect in the most elegant of costly widow's weeds. Her face was a clear oval, cream tinged with pink, and her large dark eyes looked upon us imploringly under smooth translucent lids. In Dr. Johnson's plain old-fashioned sitting room, she looked like a white butterfly momentarily hovering over the gnarled bole of an oak tree.

Dr. Sam: Johnson, *detector* of crime and chicane, and friend to the distrest, bowed over the small white hand. Then in his sixty-third year, tall and burly, aukward and uncouth, he yet valued himself upon his complaisance to the ladies. His large but shapely fingers engulfed the dainty digits of our guest as he led her to an armed chair, the while replying:

" 'Twere duty, no less. But first, ma'am (seating

her), you must tell me how you came to lose the child. Pray attend, Mr. Boswell, I shall value your opinion. Ma'am, I present Mr. Boswell, advocate, of Edinburgh in Scotland, my young friend and favourite companion."

Smiling with pleasure to hear myself thus described, I bowed low. The lady inclined slightly, and began her story:

"My son, Sir Richard Claybourne, is no child. He is in his twenty-seventh year, if—if he is in life. His father, Sir Hubert Claybourne, of Claybourne Hall in Kent, left me inconsolable ten years ago, and our only son, Richard, then sixteen, acceded to the title and estate.

"Well, sir, 'tis a common story. Tho' we had been close before, once he came into his estate, I could not controul him. Claybourne Hall saw him but seldom, for he preferred raking in London, running from the gaming tables to—to places more infamous yet.

"Then, as he approached his majority," the soft voice went on, "Richard fell deeply in love, and proposed to marry. 'Twas against my wishes, for tho' the young lady's fortune was ample, she was brought up in a household where I, alas, have no friends. But being neighbours, Cynthia Wentworth drew Richard home to Kent, and at Claybourne, on a day in spring, they were wedded and bedded.

"Alas the day! That very night, Richard burst into my chamber, where I lay alone waking and fretting. He was dishevelled and wild, and, Damn the bitch, says he (pardon me, gentlemen), she has broken my heart, I shall leave England this night, I'll go for a soldier, and never return while she lives. Nothing I said could disswade him. Take care of Claybourne estate, cried he to me, and was gone."

The low voice faltered, and went on:

"With the help of Mr. Matthew Rollis, my trusted solicitor, I kept up the estate. Cynthia Wentworth, mute and grim, went back to her foster folk at Rendle. No word came from Richard; but enquiring of returning soldiers, once or twice I heard a rumor of him in the New World, at New-York, at Jamaica. Since then, nothing. Six years have now passed. I can bear it no longer. I must find my boy."

Dr. Johnson looked grave.

" 'Tis long for a voluntary absence. Who is the next heir? Who had an interest to prevent Sir Richard's return?"

"Good lack, Dr. Johnson, you do not think—?"

"I do not think. I ask meerly."

"You alarm me, sir. The next heir is Jeremy Claybourne, a lad now rising twenty. He springs from the Claybournes of Rendle, a family I have long lived at enmity with. His father, my husband's late brother Hector—well, I say nothing of him; he was kind to me while he lived. But his wife was a venomous vixen, and never spared to vilify me. In that house Cynthia was brought up and her mind poisoned against me. On them I blame the whole affair.

"Indeed it is pressure from that quarter that drives me to action. The lawyers will have Richard declared dead, and his cousin Jeremy put in possession. On that day they will turn me out into the world without a friend. He must come home and protect me."

"Then we must find him. You say your son departed on his wedding night. How did he depart?"

"I know not how, sir, but Claybourne estate is on the coast; I have thought he went by sea, perhaps in some smuggler's vessel."

"A course full of peril," commented my friend, who considered that being in a ship was like being in gaol, with the likelihood of being drowned. "Alas, madam, what assures you that he is still in life?"

"A mother's heart! I *know* that, somewhere, he is alive!"

"Then we must appeal to him to shew himself, wherever he may be. Bozzy, your tablets. By your leave, ma'am, we'll address him thus in all the papers (dictating):

SIR RICHARD CLAYBOURNE went from his Friends in the year '66, & left his Mother bereft & his Affairs in disorder. Whosoever makes known his whereabouts shall be amply rewarded & he himself is implored to return to the Bosom of his grieving Mother.

Claybourne Hall in Kent
April ye 10th, 1772

"There, madam, let this simple screed be disseminated, especially in the seaports of the New World, where he was last heard of; and my life upon it, if he be alive, Sir Richard will give over his sulks and return to his duties."

"I pray it may be so," murmured my Lady.

Dr. Johnson looked after the crested coach as it left the court, and shook his head.

"Let us all pray, for her sake, it may be so."

Time passed. I returned to Edinburgh, and quite forgot the problem of the missing Sir Richard Claybourne and his whereabouts; until once more, in th spring of 1773, I visited London.

I was sitting comfortably with my learned friend in his house in Johnson's Court, when a billet was handed in. Dr. Johnson put up his well-shaped brows as he read it, and passed it to me.

> "By the grace of Heaven, Sir Richard Claybourne is found!
>
> Come at once to the Cross Keys.
>
> P. Claybourne
>
> at the Cross Keys,
> Wednesday, 10 of ye clock"

"I suppose we must go," said Dr. Johnson.

Wild horses would not have kept me away. We found Lady Claybourne in the wainscotted room abovestairs at the Cross Keys, sitting by the fire in a state of agitation. By her side, in silent concern, stood a grave, smooth-faced person in a decent grey coat. He proved to be Mr. Rollis, the manager of the Claybourne estate. My Lady started up at our advent.

"O bless you, Dr. Johnson, your screed has brought my Richard home to me!"

"Is he here?"

"Not yet. He is but now come into port, and gives me the rendezvous here."

"That is so," murmured Mr. Rollis in a low caressing voice, seating her gently.

"Then, my Lady, how are you sure it is he?" asked Dr. Johnson gravely.

"Old Bogie says so."

"And who is old Bogie?"

"My son's bodyservant from his childhood. To this trusted retainer I gave the task of disseminating your screed in the New World. You understand, Dr. Johnson, I am of French extraction, and come from the island of Haiti, where I still possess estates. There Bogie was born and bred, and there, his task done, he was instructed to await developments."

"And there he found Richard?"

"Sir, strolling in the gardens at Port au Prince, by chance he comes face to face with Richard. What, 'tis Bogie! cries Richard. Master Dickie! cries Bogie, and they embrace. In letters sent before, they describe this affecting scene."

"Indeed, my Lady, so they do," asseverated Rollis.

What more these letters imported was not revealed, for just then there was a knock at the door, and two men appeared on the threshold. One of them, a little old Negro with such a face as might have been carven on a walnut shell, was but a shadow behind the shoulder of the other. On this one all eyes fixed.

We saw a tall young man, dark tanned and very thin. His swarthy face, tho' gaunt and worn, yet strikingly resembled my Lady's about the eyes, which were brilliant and dark, with smooth deep lids under arching brows. He smiled her very smile, his delicately cut mouth, so like hers, flashing white teeth. His own dark hair was gathered back with a thong. His right sleeve hung empty.

The length of a heartbeat the room was poised in silence. Then my Lady rose slowly to her feet.

" 'Tis Richard," she whispered.

"Aye, 'tis Richard," murmured Rollis.

" 'Tis Richard: but O Heaven, how changed!"

In an instant the tall young man went to her, and she gathered him to her bosom. Let us draw the veil over a mother's transports.

After these sacred moments, Richard made known to us his story.

"I went from England," he said, "resolved never to return. But I soon tired of the soldier's restless life, and I resolved to seek some idyllic shade, far from the haunts of man, and there forget the past. From Jamaica I made my way to Haiti. With forged letters and a false name I obtained employment from our own factor on our own plantation. There all went on to a wish, marred only when in the late earthquake I was pinned by a fallen lintel, which paralyzed my right arm (touching the empty sleeve). Alas, Mother, I have brought you back the half of a man."

"Not so!" cried my Lady stoutly. "The arm is there. (So it was, close-clipped to his side within his fustian coat.) We'll have the best surgeons to it, and it shall mend!"

"Meanwhile," he smiled, "you shall see how my left hand serves."

To proof, he took her white fingers in his brown ones, and kissed them the while my Lady melted in smiles.

"Tho' 'twas my intent never to return," he went on, "your eloquent appeal, making its way to me, moved my heart towards England."

"The thanks be yours, Dr. Johnson," uttered my Lady.

"Aye, our thanks to you," seconded Rollis.

"And so I came down to Port au Prince, with intent to take ship, and there at the dock I met with dear Bogie—"

The black man bowed, and wiped a tear with the heel of a dusky pink palm.

"—and here I am!"

"There will be rejoicing at Claybourne," smiled my Lady. "You must be present, Dr. Johnson, Mr. Boswell."

Assenting, we parted with a promise to visit the Hall for the coming festivities of the Claybourne Dole on St. George's Day.

It was April, with spring in the air. We proceeded forthwith into Kent, tho' not to Claybourne Hall. Dr. Johnson had a mind first to visit friends at Kentish Old Priory, hard by.

Our welcome at the Priory, and our diversions thereat, form no part of this tale, except insofar as diversion was afforded at every social gathering by speculation upon the romantick, recrudescence of Sir Richard Claybourne. Those who had caught a glimpse of him importantly expatiated on his resemblance to his lady mother. Some even saw in him a look of his late father, Sir Hubert. Others again thought he resembled nobody, and suspected my Lady had been bamboozled by an imposter. She was just asking to be bamboozled, added certain cynics; while the sentimental joyed to share the bliss of a mother's heart.

As to myself, being a lawyer I took it upon me to expatiate in all companies on the great principle of filiation, by which the romantick Douglas Cause had been newly won: that, in brief, if a mother declares *This is my son*, it is so.

Heedless, the young ladies would twitter the while over the folk at Rendle. How were they taking it? How would Cynthia receive the return of her long-lost bridegroom? What would Jeremy say, now that his cousin had returned to cut him out?

As the group around the tea table was enjoyably speculating thus, one afternoon, a servant announced:

"Lady Claybourne. Mr. Claybourne."

At the names silence fell, and every head turned. Into the silence stepped a blonde girl in sea-green tissue, snug at her slender waist, and draping softly over a swaying hoop. Her sunny hair was lightly piled up à la Pompadour. There was pride in her carriage, and reserve in her level blue gaze and faint smile.

Attending her, nay, hovering over her, came a broad-shouldered youth in mulberry, whose carelessly ribbanded tawny hair, square jaw, and challenging hazel eye delineated a very John Bull in the making.

Thus I encountered at last Cynthia, Lady Claybourne, whom Richard had loved and left, and Jeremy Claybourne, his cousin and heir.

Constraint fell on the tea table. After a few observes on the weather (very fair for April), the company dispersed. The Claybournes lingered, having come of purpose to bespeak Dr. Johnson's advice in the matter of the claimant at Claybourne Hall.

"They say you have met this person," said Cynthia. "I have not. Tell me, is he Richard indeed?"

"Of course he is not!" uttered Jeremy angrily.

"The great principle of filiation—" I began.

"As you say, Mr. Boswell: the mother avers it is her son. Moreover," added Dr. Johnson, "the man of business says it is Richard; and the old-time servant asserts it is Richard."

"My Lady's too tender heart is set on the fellow," growled Jeremy, "and everybody knows Rollis and

Bogie will never gainsay her. She has them under her spell with her coaxing ways: as she has everybody. Only my mother saw thro' her. Cupidity, wilfulness, adultery, bastardy—in such terms my mother spoke of her."

"Enough, Jeremy," said Cynthia quickly, "your mother ever spoke more than she knew about her sister Claybourne."

"Never defend Lady Claybourne," muttered Jeremy, "for she is no friend to you."

"Yet Richard loved me," said the girl. "Can he be Richard, and never come near me?"

"Yet, my dear—if he left you in anger?" murmured Dr. Johnson.

"That is between me and Richard," said Cynthia stiffly.

"Then there's no more to be said."

"Oh, but there is," countered Cynthia quickly. "I'll not see Jeremy dispossessed by a pretender. Pray, Dr. Johnson, will you not scrutinize this fellow, and detect whether he be Richard indeed, or an imposter?"

"Why, if he be an imposter, 'tis my hand in the business has raised him up," observed Dr. Johnson. "I'll scan him narrowly, you may be sure. But why do you not confront him yourself?"

"The door is closed against me."

"We'll confront him at the Dole," said Jeremy grimly.

"What is this Claybourne Dole we hear so much about?" I enquired curiously.

"Sir," replied Cynthia, " 'tis a whimsy from the Dark Ages, of a death-bed vow to relieve the poor forever, and a death-bed curse, that if 'tis neglected, the Claybourne line shall fail. For six years past Jeremy, as the heir, has upheld the custom; and all Claybournes, even I must play their part on St. George's Day."

"Which is this day week," remarked Dr. Johnson. "Well, well, I'll note Sir Richard's proceedings in the meantime."

Next day, according to our invitation at the Cross Keys, we became guests at Claybourne Hall. We found the Hall to be a stately Palladian mansion, with classical pilasters and myriad sashwindows taking the light. Here the dowager Lady Claybourne reigned in splendour, and now that her Richard was beside her, all was love and abundance.

Richard indeed moved as one waking out of a dream, from the formal garden to the bluffs above the sea, from the great hall to the portrait gallery. As he stared at the likenesses of his ancestors in the latter, we were enabled to stare at him, as a youth on canvas, as a man in the flesh. As my Lady had said, how changed!

The youthful face in the portrait was smooth and high-coloured. The face of flesh was now thin and sallow. But in both countenances, the fresh and the worn, the look of my Lady was apparent in the large thin-lidded eyes and the curve of lip. In the portrait, young Richard rested his left hand on the hilt of his sword, and held in his right the bridle of his favourite horse.

"Gallant Soldier, remember, mother?" murmured Richard. "He bade fair to be the fastest horse in the county."

"He is so still. You shall ride him yet, my son, when the arm mends."

Following her glance, I perceived that the useless arm had been coaxed into its sleeve, and saw in the hand the ball of crimson wool whereby, with continual kneading and plying, the atrophied muscles were to be, by little and little, restored to use. The slack fingers with an effort tightened about the crimson wool and loosed it again, tightened and loosed.

"I'll ride Gallant Soldier yet," vowed Sir Richard.

Meanwhile, the swift steed was Richard's delight and wherever he went, out of doors in the fresh April weather, horse and groom were sure to be near him.

The out of doors was Richard's element. The old gamekeeper rejoiced to have him back, and marvelled at his undiminished skill, tho' with the left hand, at angling and fencing and shooting with the pistol; tho' the sporting gun was no longer within his power.

Indoors, other times, the restored Sir Richard would be busied with Mr. Rollis, turning over old deeds or signing new ones, as to the manor born. Mr. Rollis exclaimed in wonder, that the new signature, tho' left-handed, so closely resembled the old.

In certain respects, methought, the long sojourn in the wilds shewed its effects. The skin was leather-tanned by the furnace of the West Indies. The voice was harsh, and so far from smacking of his upbringing in Kent, the manner of speech had a twang that spoke of the years in Haiti.

At table, also, the heir's manners, to my way of thinking, left something to be desired. But what can a man do who must feed himself with one hand? Old Bogie hovered ever at his shoulder, ready to cut his meat; while at his knee, rolling adoring eyes, sat Richard's old dog, a cross fat rug of a thing named Gypsy. I noticed she got more than her share of titbits.

Only once during that week was the name of Cynthia mentioned, when Dr. Johnson took opportunity to say:

"Sir, will you not see your wife?"

Richard shook his head.

"Not yet. Do not ask it. Let me mend first."

"Cynthia's suspense must be painful," observed Dr. Johnson.

Wherever Richard was, my Lady was sure to be close at hand. Now she came between to say coldly:

"Cynthia has Jeremy to console her. Let her alone."

Richard turned away in silence.

St. George's Day, April 23, 1773, dawned fair. Claybourne Hall hummed and was redolent with final preparations. At the farther edge of the south meadow they were roasting whole oxen, and putting up long tables on trestles to set forth the viands to come. At the near end a platform under a red and white stripéd canopy offered shelter against sun or shower, whatever April weather might ensue.

At the Hall as morning advanced, Lady Claybourne bustled about; but Richard did not appear. Soon he would face his first meeting with the world. How would he be received?

At mid-morning, we all attended Sir Richard's levee in the old-fashioned way. A rainbow of splendid garments had been kept furbished for him from his raking days. For this great occasion, he chose a suit of cream brocaded and laced with gold, in which he looked like a bridegroom. A modish new wig with high powdered fore-top well became his flashing dark eyes and haggard face. In this he shewed his only trace of foppery, the outmoded hats and wigs of past days having been condemned *en masse,* and new ones bespoke from London.

My Lady, too, was adorned most like a bride, for she had given over her mourning weeds upon Richard's return, and now wore silver tissue edged with bullion lace. As to me, I had donned my bloom-coloured coat, while Dr. Johnson was satisfied to be decent in chestnut broadcloth.

On the stroke of noon we issued forth to greet the quality and commonalty already gathering to honour the day. Richard vibrated like a wire; my Lady, glowing with joy, never left his side. Thus, strolling in the meadow, we exchanged bows with the neighbouring squires, and nodded condescendingly to the assembling tenantry. Sometimes Richard ut-

tered a name; sometimes he only made a leg, bowed
and smiled. His eyes shewed the strain he was under.

As we strolled, suddenly my Lady took in a sibilant breath, and gripped her son's fingers. Two persons stood in our way. Richard uttered one word:
"Cynthia!"

Her hand on Jeremy's, the girl stood and eyed the
speaker, utterly still. At last she spoke:

"Who are you?"

"I am Sir Richard Claybourne, your humble servant, and your husband that was."

She searched him deep, the sallow face, the dark
eyes, the useless arm.

"Make me believe it," she said. "Answer me but
three questions."

"Not now," snapped Lady Claybourne. "The
Dole begins."

"I think you must, Sir Richard," said Dr. Johnson
gently.

"Very well, sir. But think well, Cynthia, you may
not like the answers."

"If true, I shall like them very well. One: when we
began our loves (the clear skin rosied), what was my
name for you?"

"Dickon," said the claimant instantly.

"No, 'Rich,' you are wrong. Now say: where was
our secret post office?"

"In a hollow tree."

"That is true. Which one?"

"Ah, that I have forgotten."

"Never mind. Why did you leave me as you did?"

"You know why."

"I know why. Do you?"

"I beg you, Cynthia, spare me saying it."

"I do not fear to hear it."

Eyes downcast, Richard uttered low: "You force me to say it. Because I found you to be used goods."

Jeremy doubled his fists and aimed a blow, which Richard swiftly fended with his own.

"Stand back, Jeremy," said Cynthia coolly: "he knows he lies."

Jeremy, muttering, dropped his arms, and the claimant followed suit, as the dowager cried:

"Of course the little trollop must deny it. Enough of this farce!"

"Answer me but this, if you be Richard," pursued Cynthia steadily, "what did you say in your farewell note?"

"An unworthy trick, Cynthia, I left you no farewell note."

"Shall I shew it you?"

"I forbid it!" cried the dowager angrily. " 'Tis clear Cynthia will tell any lie, pass any forgery, to do away with you and get the estate for Jeremy. Come, begin the Dole!"

She swept Richard away. At her gesture, he mounted the platform and spoke:

"My people—my dear friends, companions of my youth! Richard is returned, and we shall have better days at Claybourne Hall. I am too moved to say more."

A silence. Would they reject him? Then the cheer burst forth: *Huzza!* It was Mr. Rollis who gave the triple "Hip hip!"

Bowing, the master of Claybourne reached his hand to his lady mother, and descended to the level. Old Bogie with a basket of loaves and Mr. Rollis with a purse of crown pieces fell in on either side. Jeremy and Cynthia, stiff-backed, followed; and we, Sir Richard's guests, brought up the rear.

Drawn up before the dais, shepherded by friends and relations in gala array, stood two dozen hand-picked and hand-scrubbed antients of days. Clean smocks cloathed the toothless gaffers, and snowy aprons adorned the silver-haired gammers. The Dole began: to each, a gracious word from Sir Richard, a crown piece from Rollis's purse, and a fat brown loaf from Bogie's basket.

The entourage had gone part way down the line, when a boy with a billet pushed through the crowd and handed the folded paper to Sir Richard. The latter snapped it open, read, and scowled. Then he shrugged, threw down the crumpled paper (which in the interest of neatness I retrieved and pocketed for future destruction) and stepped forward to the next curtseying old crone.

There was still bread in the basket and silver in the purse when again a newcomer pushed his way importantly through the crowd. I recognized the burly fellow with his staff and his writ: the parish constable, come as I supposed to bear his part in the drama of the Claybourne Dole. At sight of him,

Richard stopped stock-still. Then he bowed abruptly, and strode swiftly away. We saw him reach the edge of the meadow, where as usual the favourite steed, Gallant Soldier, saddled and bridled, stood with his groom. The Dole party stood and gaped as Richard leaped to the saddle, slapped the reins two-handed, and tore off at a gallop.

As we stood staring the dowager rounded on Cynthia.

"You wicked, wicked girl!" she cried. "Now what have you done! You have driven Richard from home a second time!"

"Be that as it may," said Dr. Johnson, "continue the Dole, Sir Jeremy, lest the Curse fall upon you."

Under his commanding eye, the Dole party re-formed about Jeremy. I noticed that the constable, stately with writ and staff, belatedly brought up the rear; and so the Dole was completed.

Cheering, the tenantry broke ranks and attacked the tables; but there was no feasting for us. Marshalled by Dr. Johnson, we found ourselves indoors in the withdrawing room, sitting about on the stiff brocaded chairs as the late sunlight slanted in along the polished floor. We seemed to sit most like a select committee, myself and Cynthia and Jeremy, Lady Claybourne and Rollis and Bogie, with Dr. Johnson as it were in the chair; and the constable like a sergeant-at-arms, solidly established just outside the door.

"Where is Sir Richard?" demanded Mr. Rollis.

"Vanished," replied Dr. Johnson with a broad

smile. "We have put the genie back in the bottle."

"How do you know he is vanished?"

"Because 'twas I conjured him away."

"Alas for my Lady!" cried generous-hearted Cynthia, "to lose her son a second time."

With a heart-broken gesture, Lady Claybourne put her kerchief to her eyes.

"Save your sympathy, she has not lost him," said Dr. Johnson calmly.

"Unravel this mystery, sir," exclaimed Cynthia.

"I have not all the strands in my fingers, but the master string I have pulled, and the unravelling begins. You have heard the cynical saying, if you should send word to every member of Parliament, *Fly, all is discovered*, the floor would be half empty next day."

In a trice I had out of my pocket the note the claimant had thrown down. *Fly, all is discovered*, it read.

"But he did not fly," I objected.

"Not then," conceded my friend. "But upon the heels of the warning came the constable with his staff and a great writ in his hand—instructed by me, I confess—and that did the business. The false Richard is off, and I venture to suppose he'll not return."

"How could you be so sure he was not the true Richard?" I asked curiously.

"Sir, the affair of Susanna and the elders was my first hint. As the lying elders could not say with one voice under which tree she sinned, so there was no agreement on the scene of that romantick meeting with old Bogie, whether the gardens or the docks. Was there such a meeting? It occurred to me to doubt it. Yet the positive voices of all three, mother, man of business, and old servant, overbore me for the nonce."

"Not to mention," said I, "the devotion of the dog Gypsy at Claybourne."

"Cupboard love," smiled Johnson. "Had you fed her, she would have drooled in *your* lap. No, the dog did not move me. For at Claybourne, I was again observing matter for doubt. There was, for instance, the affair of the wigs and hats. The false Richard wore his predecessor's garments very well. But the headgear would not fit; he was obliged to obtain a new supply."

"Moreover," my friend continued, "the real Sir Richard was right-handed. The sword in his portrait was scabbarded to the left, as it must be for a right-handed man to draw. But I soon perceived this fellow was always left-handed. He wrote, he shot, he fished left-handed with the perfect ease of a lifetime. Therefore must his right arm seem to be stricken. Then if he had learned from someone to write like Sir Richard, yet perforce not perfectly, the shift of hand explains all. Thus too, the arm must seem to mend. Who would willingly go one-armed forever?"

"And it mended miraculously," added Jeremy drily, "when I struck at him and he struck back two-fisted."

"So I saw," remarked Dr. Johnson, "tho' 'twas over in the blink of an eye. Yet it shook him, and Cynthia's tests still worse, making him all the more ready to believe *All is discovered*, and fly at once, by that mount he had always ready."

"Then where is the real Sir Richard?" I put the question that was hanging in the air.

"Ah, there's the question," said Dr. Johnson. "Let us ask Cynthia. Forgive me, my dear, do not answer unless you will; but had you really a note of farewell?"

"I will answer," said Cynthia in a low voice, "for Jeremy has the right to know. There was a note of farewell left for me in our hollow tree." Reaching into her bodice, she brought it forth. "Here it is."

With compressed lips, Lady Claybourne turned away. Three heads bent over the yellowing scrap. The message we read was brief and bitter:

"Now you know me, I am unworthy to touch you, But be comforted, you shall be rid of your incubus when the tide goes out. Farewell, for you'll never see me more.

                                        Rich"

"I made sure he had thrown himself into the sea," whispered Cynthia.

"Dear heart," cried Jeremy, "on his wedding night, why would he so?"

"Because," said Cynthia, low, "he came to me with the French disease, and left me rather than infect me. He was half mad with remorse and drink taken, and I feared what he might do. 'Twas pure relief when I heard his mother had seen him and set him on his way."

"But had she?" asked Johnson gravely. "—Sit down, Lady Claybourne. You need not answer. I will answer for you. You never saw Richard that night. He was drowned. But you were determined still to rule Claybourne estate, and you had the wit and the will to invent a story to keep you there tho' Richard was gone. How long, think you, Cynthia, could she have remained, had you displayed this everlasting farewell?"

"I was but fourteen, and I wanted so to believe," murmured Cynthia. "But now—I know not."

"Perhaps," said Dr. Johnson, turning a stern face on the old Negro, "perhaps Bogie knows."

The dark eyes darted left and right. No sign came from my Lady, but Jeremy spoke with gruff gentleness:

"Speak up, Bogie. Tell us the truth; it shall not be held against you."

"I know," whispered the black painfully. "When Sir Richard was gone, none knew whither, I was set to search, and so 'twas I found at the cliff top his wedding coat folded, and a note held down by a stone."

"What said the note? Or can you not read?"

"I can read. It began: Honoured Mother, When you read this I shall be dead—"

Cynthia hid her face in her hands.

"I read no more," went on Bogie, "but took coat and note to my Lady in her chamber. She read it

dry-eyed, and mused long. At last Bogie, says she, I
learn by this billet that your young master has left
England, and we are to keep all things in readiness
for his return. Was I to gainsay her?"

Lady Claybourne sat like a figure carved in ice.

"Yet Sir Richard would never return," went on
Dr. Johnson, "and Jeremy's guardians became more
and more pressing. I suggest that as Jeremy approached his majority, a scheam was conceived to
hold the estate, a scheam in which you three—you,
my Lady, and Rollis and Bogie—had your parts to
play."

"And you too, Dr. Johnson," smiled Rollis, un-
abashed.

"And I too," said the philosopher wryly. "My part
was to be the dupe, and lend my authority to the
comedy of 'The Return of the Long Lost Heir.'
'Twas all too pat. He will be found, predicts my
Lady like a sybil, and found he is, on her own
ground, in Haiti. How? Because—as I now perceive—she arranged it—through a trusted mes-
senger, her old slave from Haiti, our friend Mr.
Bogie. Well, Bogie?"

The old man almost smiled as he inclined his
head.

"But who was he, then, whom Bogie found in
Haiti," I demanded, "so miraculously suited to the
part?"

"I know not," replied Dr. Johnson; "but I can
guess. I think we shall find that there was someone
in Haiti whom my Lady sent there out of the way

long ago; someone whom she would gladly establish for life at Claybourne Hall; someone who so closely resembled her that he could win wide acceptance as the lost heir. To speak plainly: her son."

"Her *son?*"

"Her bastard son, Sir Jeremy, whose existence your mother railed at in years past. Is that not so, Lady Claybourne?"

My Lady disdained to answer.

"Is that not so, Mr. Rollis?"

"That is so, Dr. Johnson," Mr. Rollis smiled thinly. "The lad was troublesome, and 'twas I who secretly shipped him off for her to the Haiti plantation. Thither my Lady sent Bogie, to instruct him and bring him back. Bogie is not as simple as he seems. Come, my Lady, say this is so, for our best course now is to compound the matter with Sir Jeremy."

"Compound, will you?" said Jeremy darkly. "I'll look to the strong-box first."

"As to the strong-box," said Rollis calmly, "you may set your mind at rest, for I have kept the keys. Tho' in indifferent matters I was ruled by my Lady—"

"D'you call it an indifferent matter, raising me up a false husband!" cried Cynthia indignantly.

"As to that," returned the solicitor coolly, "I never expected my Lady's mad scheam to prevail; and as to the estate, I have kept it faithfully for whoever comes after."

"What impudence!" cried Jeremy. "Dr. Johnson,

say, shall we not give these conspirators into cus-
tody, and send after the fleeing imposter?"

Lady Claybourne spoke for the first time:

"He'll hang for it. Would you hang your brother,
Jeremy?"

"My *brother*?"

"Your father's son."

"Of the blood on both sides!" exclaimed Dr.
Johnson. "Small wonder he passed for the heir!"

"And small wonder my mother railed," added
Jeremy.

"Sir Jeremy will not desire a scandal at
Claybourne," said my Lady with perfect calm. "He
will prefer that I should take my dower right and
withdraw to Haiti. My son Paul—whom, as you say,
I have not lost—shall join me. Now I will bid you
good night. Come, Rollis. Come, Bogie."

" 'Tis for the best. Let it be so, Sir Jeremy," said
my wise friend.

My Lady, head held high, sailed out at the door,
and Rollis and Bogie followed.

"Be it so," assented Jeremy gravely, and the constable let them pass. "Now," he went on, his face
softening, "there is but one more word to say.
Cynthia (taking her hand)—Lady Claybourne, will
you wed with me, and be Lady Claybourne still?"

"Yes, Jeremy," said Cynthia.

[The 18th Century had its claimants, its "lost heirs," notably James Annesley (1743) and Archibald Douglas (1767); but this story reflects neither. It may suggest rather the mystery of the Tichborne claimant a century later. You may recognize Lady Tichborne and Old Bogle and the Tichborne Dole; you may read Australia for Haiti; you may even discern a plausible explanation of the many inexplicable features of that puzzling affair. In certain fictitious elements, of course, including the outcome, my story differs widely from the Tichborne case.

The best book on the Tichborne mystery is Douglas Woodruff's *The Tichborne Claimant* (New York: Farrar, Straus and Cudahy, 1957).]

THE RESURRECTION MEN

"Body-snatchers and Resurrection Men, 'tis a scandal!" growled Dr. Sam: Johnson in his loud bull's mutter.

"Oranges! Sweet Chaney oranges!"

The call of the orange-girl rose, filling the theatre in the interval between the tragedy and the after-piece. It was at the after-piece that my philosophical friend had taken umbrage, for it was announced as *The Resurrection of Harlequin Deadman*, a theme which Dr. Johnson considered both sacrilegious and inopportune.

"What are these mountebanks thinking of," he demanded, "to give us another dead man, when the whole town reeks with the grave and the vault, when ghouls and Resurrection Men lift our dead from the earth (shuddering) to be sacked and carried off by night, and carved like mutton by the Anatomist in the morning!"

"Oranges! Sweet oranges!"

The orange-girl was before us, a trim little piece

with a dimple beside her bee-stung lip. I longed much to try her mettle, but set up there on publick view, so to speak, in a forward box at Drury Lane Theatre, between two weighty and well-known personages, I hesitated, and she passed on.

Dr. Sam: Johnson, burly and broad, his little brown wig clapped carelessly askew on his head, was known to every tavern and tea-table in town as Ursa Major, the Great Bear, the Grand Cham of Literature.

Our companion, Mr. Saunders Welch, tall, robust, and powerful, with his snowy poll and his round benevolent face, was recognized by the upper and the under world alike as the incorruptible Westminster magistrate, second in command to the Blind Beak of Bow Street himself. Often had the world seen him leading the procession to a Tyburn hanging, black-clad, stately on his white horse, bearing his black baton of office tipped with silver.

Nor was I, I flatter myself, unknown on the London scene: James Boswell, Esq:, of Auchinleck in Scotland, advocate and man of the world, chronicler of the *detections* of Dr. Sam: Johnson: very much at your service. Many an eye from the stalls was marking my elegant bloom-coloured attire, my swarthy visage set off by powdered clubbed wig, my genteel bearing and complaisant air.

"And what does Bow Street," my worthy friend was demanding, "to quell these grave-robbing scoundrels?"

"What can Bow Street do?" rumbled Mr. Welch.

"These involuntary levitations of inhumated decedents—" He paused impressively, for he loved to outdo Dr. Sam: Johnson himself in the matter of sesquipedalian terminology.

"By which you mean, digging up the dead?" suggested Johnson with a half smile.

"Just so, sir. We do what we can to prevent it. The vaults are concealed, but the Resurrection Men find them out; coffins are sealed, but somehow come unsealed; guards are set, but the Resurrection Men prove stronger. They are persistent, for the traffick is very profitable. The Anatomist pays high for the fresh bodies he dissects."

"Too much of this," growled Johnson in revulsion. "Harlequin Deadman, pah! Let us go."

I had got my friend to vist the theatre by promise of a tragedy of a moral tendency, *The Distrest Mother*; and now it was over he was little disposed to wait for the harlequinade. But I found myself reluctant to leave my bee-stung charmer unattempted.

"Do, sir," I perswaded, "do sit on with us, for they say Mr. De Loutherbourg back stage has outdone himself with his scenes and his transformations, his opticks and his mechanicks, his grand effects of light and dark."

"Well, well, I'll humour you, Bozzy. Let us see what this Dutchman can do."

This complaisance enabled me to close with the pretty orange-girl, and privily purchase from her at an inflated rate not only a regale of oranges, but a rendezvous for a later hour at a bagnio hard by Covent Garden. I devoured my orange well pleased.

Suddenly, with a loud groan of the tuba, the musick banged up a grotesque dead march. Salt-box and cleaver beat time, and nimble fingers made the marrow-bones to rattle. Ropes creaked, and the scene-curtain rolled up in Mr. De Loutherbourg's new manner. The stage lay in darkness. All the candles, at the front and in the wing-ladders alike, had been snuffed. Only a large opal moon gleamed of itself in a black velvet sky.

" 'Tis some chymical substance makes it glow," observed Dr. Johnson, his interest engaged, for he dabbled in chymical experimentation himself.

The dead march swelled, torch-light appeared, and a grotesque funeral procession stalked into view. The children of the company, inappropriately attired as Cupids, capered on first, scattering flowers. Harlequin's bier was borne on shoulder high, under a diamond-chequered pall. There followed his friends and enemies as mourners, Columbine in her gauzy skirts supported by the noted Grimaldi as Pantaloon, Clown with white-painted face wringing his floury hands, and the rest of the farcical rout. Dr. Johnson snorted. He hates to be reminded that man—even Harlequin—is mortal.

Harlequin under his pall was laid in his grave—that is to say, in the Grave Trap, depressed just deep enough—and the mourners footed it off to a quickstep. De Loutherbourg's opal moon precipitously declined and set.

In the dead darkness there was a stir. A sheeted figure, gleaming with a luminous moony glow, sat up in the grave. It was startling. Ladies shrieked, men cursed in admiration. Then the figure straightened and stepped up, the glowing cerements were cast aside, and Harlequin stood before us—a skeleton! Every bone gleamed with that same mysterious moonlight glow, the palms of his hand shone, and where the face should have been shimmered the grin of a skull.

"Bravo, De Loutherbourg!" muttered Welch.

"Tschah!" said Johnson, "black body hose and bright paint!"

The musick struck up a weird melody. Wright was Harlequin that night, and his Deadman's Dance was a triumph of loose shank-bones and prodigious leaps. But Dr. Johnson, finding in it no moral content, could not sit still. When the foolery ended, we hardly stayed to hear tomorrow's bill announced *(Venice Preserved* and *Harlequin Cherokee)* before we escaped ahead of the press.

Outside the theatre, as usual, a mob of riff-raff was gathered, chairmen, link-boys, night-walking wenches, ready-handed rapparees, pimps and pickpockets.

Past us as we left the play-house strolled a youth who engaged my regard, fresh of face, erect of form, lace-ruffled, clad in ivory brocade. Striding easily forward, he came up against a knot of blackguards. There was a jostle. The boy seized a collar and shouted. I thought the word was "Murder!" He was fatally right. A knife flashed, the boy fell, the brawlers melted from sight.

"Halt!" shouted Welch, and gave chase, but in vain. They were gone.

"Zookers, my cousin!" ejaculated a flash-looking bystander in a bag-wig, starting forward. "He's in a fit! Quick, lads, bear him to the tavern!"

Several hands were reaching for the boy, when past my elbow sped a lady in rose-coloured lutestring, small and daintily formed, her grey eyes enormous in her pale delicate face.

"Stand off!" she cried, and the would-be helpers fell back.

"Patrick!" she breathed, and knelt beside him. He lay as the dead, no breath, no motion. She wrung her hands.

"My son!" she wailed. "What shall I do? He's dead as his father died, and the body-snatchers will have him as they had his father, and what will become of me?"

"Give place," said a resonant voice. "I am a surgeon, madam, John Hardiman, at your service. Pray permit me, milady."

He knelt beside her, a military-looking man of middle height. Soon he rose, shaking his head.

"Lend a hand here," he cried, "and bear him to my surgery in White Hart Yard, where I may apply my skill to restore him."

"Never!" cried the lady. "He shall go home, for my house is hard by. Summon a chair!"

"A chair for Lady Julia Fitzpatrick!" voices took up the cry.

"Who is this lady?" I wondered aloud. "And what means her talk of the bodysnatchers?"

"Why, all the world knows Lady Julia Fitzpatrick," replied Dr. Johnson, "sister to an Earl, wife to the late Fighting Fitzpatrick, the notable Irish duellist. He died last year in a brawl at a tavern, and yon boy, his son, saw him fall. The tale they tell is strange. Fitzpatrick had, they said, his heart misplaced in his breast, an opponent could never nick it. You may imagine how the Anatomist would desiderate such a rarity."

"Preposterous!" I ejaculated.

"That may be; but preposterous or no, what the world believes, as I observed in the matter of the Monboddo Ape Boy, is a sharp-edged fact upon which a man may cut himself. So it was, perhaps, with Fighting Fitzpatrick. As the story goes, an assassin, instructed by the Anatomist, put a quarrel on him and struck the right spot, ending his days and producing the desiderated cadaver. I know the Sack-em-up Men lifted him, for I saw the empty grave myself, passing by the churchyard of St.-Mark-in-the-Fields, with the coffin riven and empty and the winding-sheet thrown down beside. Small wonder if Lady Julia dreads the Resurrection Men."

"A shocking story!"

"It is so. And who knows? If Fighting Fitzpatrick proved in fact an anatomical rarity, might not the same Anatomist have a mind to have the boy on his dissecting table, to see if such misplacement runs in families?"

As we spoke thus, two burly bearers edged a sedan-chair with difficulty through the press. Many hands lifted the fallen boy, his brocades now blotched with crimson. The lady ascended the chair, received the inert form beside her, the half-door was fastened, and the chairmen heaved up the poles. The attentive surgeon walked beside.

"Let us go along," said my benevolent friend with concern, "for I perceive this lady needs a friend."

I followed along towards Covent Garden; but I had another kind of friend waiting in a bagnio there, and at Lady Julia's door in Russell Street I parted for the night.

Frustration ensued. My little Cytherean with the dimple, after all, embezzled my gold and left me standing, no doubt following some deeper purse to a more fashionable bagnio; and thus she passes from my story. I went late to my lodging in an evil mood, slept but ill, and rose to melancholy. Then when I called in Bolt Court, looking for the consolations of philosophy, Dr. Johnson was from home.

Not until evening did we meet. We dined together at the Mitre. I was silent as to the perfidious orange-girl; but over a mighty cut off the joint, my benevolent friend adverted to the tragedy at the theatre, and imparted something of its consequences.

"At my urging," he remarked with satisfaction,

"little Davy Garrick at Drury Lane has consented to lay upon the shelf the resurrection of Harlequin Deadman as long as the publick is shocked by the doings of the real Resurrection Men."

"And what of the bereaved mother, Lady Julia?"

"Calling in Russell Street, I found her resolved that these ghouls shll not have the remains of Patrick. She fears that they may snatch him from the very house of mourning, and perhaps justly so, for certain it is, that it was a body-snatcher's trick, almost successful, when yon bravo in the bag-wig claimed kin and would have carried him off but for Lady Julia's arrival. She is made wary. The body has been shrouded and coffined, and the lid made fast, by her own hands. The wake is in progress, and in the morning the body will be consigned to earth, to be kept under strong guard while the cadaver is fresh. Pah! It destroys the appetite!"

My sturdy friend, falling silent, applied an undestroyed appetite to the demolishing of a toothsome veal pye. I lent a hand. Not 'til it was consumed did he lean back with a sigh.

"Come, then, Mr. Boswell, we are expected at Lady Julia's."

"What, sir, will *you* make one at a wake, and join in the pillaloo or Irish howl?"

"I will do more than that for a distrest mother."

We found Lady Julia's house decked in deep mourning. Sable crape draped the doorway and muffled the knocker. The door was opened to us by a sombre-clad footman with a pugnacious bog-trotter's face, and we stood in an entrance hall hung from ceiling to floor with rich mourning trappings laced with silver. From within sounded the low moans and loud howls of the Irish pillaloo.

"Dr. Johnson, Mr. Boswell, your servant!"

It was the undertaker, swelling and grand in black broadcloth.

"What, good Mr. Blackstock, sir, yours!"

The man was known to us, for we had met at Dilly's, under more congenial circumstances. Mr. Blackstock, the society undertaker, broad in the shoulder and short in the leg, had a face that reminded me of that pair of Greek masks, one broad grin alternating with a professional countenance of distress. He wore the latter now, mouth corners turned down and eyes turned up.

"A sad occasion, sir," he intoned; "and," he added in a confidential murmur, "a strange one. These Irish are too much for me! No expense spared on trappings of woe—" He glanced with approval at the costly velvet hangings. "—night made hideous by heathenish howlings—" The pillaloo rose to a loud keen, wavered, and fell. "No wax figure to display as in my father's time; no hatchment, no loved countenance preserved through my art; but shrouded, coffined and screwed down in haste, and hugger-mugger off to the grave in the morning! I'll never understand the Irish!"

"Lady Julia is apprehensive for the safety of the remains," remarked Dr. Johnson. "And she has cause, sir, she has cause."

Mr. Blackstock looked put about.

"Most unfortunate, that, sir, last year," he muttered, "but I did all I could, the usual guards at the grave, spring-guns, and so on; and so I shall again, with close supervision too. Lady Julia may make herself easy."

"I will tell her so," said Dr. Johnson.

Mr. Blackstock bent his weeds in a bow that would have done honour to an archbishop, and we passed withinside.

In a parlour hung with black, the coffin stood dark, covered with a rich sable velvet pall. Candles flickered at head and foot. Around it knelt the inferior Irish females of the household, tearing at their dishevelled locks and ululating with a will. Even ladies of the better sort moaned into their pocket handkerchiefs, and gentlemen stood by looking grave. A strong posse of rough-cut Irish footmen put about the consoling glass, and often retired to the kitchen, there presumably to console themselves with similar potations.

In all the hullabaloo, little Lady Julia sat erect, silent, dry-eyed and grim. To my surprise, Dr. Hardiman the surgeon had ingratiated himself, for he stood by her, gently smiling, with hartshorn bottle at the ready, and when her duties called her away, he supported her steps.

With doleful countenance, Mr. Blackstock tiptoed softly among us, distributing the trappings of woe. Elaborate "weepers," white bows fluttering fringe, soon adorned every arm. Rich mourning garments were passed out, black shammy gloves, Italian crape hat-bands, silk mourning scarves, and the finest of funereal cloaks, black broadcloth from neck to heel, and deep-hooded, to hide the ravages of tears. Tearless, the bereaved mother submitted to be swathed in a long black crape veil.

As the candles paled with the waning of night, the bearers shouldered the coffin and bore it out in the grey of dawn. At the door six black horses waited with the hearse, of carved wood black-painted, and surmounted by a sooty solemn crest of tall nodding feathers. The coffin was slid in. We mounted the mourning coaches, and the cortège paced off to the tolling of the church bells, bearing the slain boy to his resting-place in the churchyard of St.-Mark-in-the-Fields.

St. Mark is no longer in the fields, for the city has moved out that way; but the churchyard still extends alongside, massy wall, ivied lych-gate, solemn yew-tree, old grey tombstones, all very fit for our melancholy obsequies.

Of the funeral sermon, whined out with a snuffle by a pursy divine, I say nothing; but at last we stood by the opened grave. A wall-eyed sexton and his muscular helper stood by, looking, I thought, rather too pleased for the nature of the occasion; but no doubt they had been well fee'd.

"Ashes to ashes, dust to dust—" The first clods fell upon the coffin, and the sexton and his man wielded spades with a will to close the grave. I wondered how soon it would be opened in unholy resurrection.

The mourning coaches departed, but a knot of us lingered: the sexton, Mr. Blackstock and his men, Mr. Saunders Welch, Dr. Johnson and myself. We remained to observe as Mr. Blackstock took his measures for the safety of the cadaver. With his own hands he set the mechanism of a wicked-looking spring-gun. As the wall-eyed sexton stacked his shovels against the wall, still grinning, two rough-clad fellows took up their post by the raw grave. Each was armed with a blunderbuss; but they looked neither intelligent nor resolute. Would they avail to stand off the body-snatchers?

My gorge rose as I imagined to myself the horrid scene—the loose earth shovelled away in hurried silence in the dark of the moon, the rending sound as the coffin is riven, the pallid form torn from its winding-sheet, huddled by brutal hands into a sack; the chink of the Anatomist's coin as he pays off the criminals, his indecent satisfaction as he bares his scalpel and carves his silent victim like butcher's meat. No endeavour, no expense, seemed too much to avoid such a fate.

These gloomy reflections haunted me as the daylight hours passed in indifferent affairs. Waiting on Dr. Johnson in Bolt Court as twilight fell, I found that he had apprehensions as gloomy. Trusting as little as I to the abilities of the fellows on guard, he proposed that we should add ourselves, unheralded, to the churchyard watch. Sore against my inclination, but much by my will, I repaired with him to St. Mark's.

There, unseen, we took up our watch in a corner of the ivy-covered church wall, where in a niche some by-gone vicar had concealed a chill stone seat in the yew-tree's dusky shade. Our mourning cloaks cloathed us from top to toe in impenetrable shadow. In the moonless night I dimly saw the shape of the fresh grave close by, where in silence the watchers passed and repassed like centinels.

As the hours rolled around, to my imagination the darkness seemed astir all around us. Vapours arose like ghosts and walked among the gravestones. Once I thought I saw a knot of cloaked figures flit through the lych-gate and silently enter the church porch. Once a black-swathed shape rose tall like a spectre behind me. My hair stood up on my head, and my tongue clove to my palate.

"Abate your horripilation, Mr. Boswell," breathed the apparition, "for I am no noctambulant, only your friend, Saunders Welch, come to bear you company."

We sat on. The church bell's solemn chime told hour upon hour. At the dead time of night, at last, a chaise drew up outside the churchyard wall. A moment later, dimly seen figures came over the wall, there was a stir by the grave-side, and we heard the whisper of shovels in loose earth.

"The body-snatchers!" I gasped. "What, sir, shall we not fall upon them?"

"No, sir. To abate this nuisance, we must take them red-handed. Let them dig."

Mr. Welch growled in his throat, but made no move. In the faint starlight, shovels swung. Piled earth rose. At last, we heard shovel strike upon plank. Then followed the shriek of riven wood. Hands reached down, and slowly the sheeted form rose out of the earth, gleaming with an eerie light. One of the body-snatchers cried out.

"Pah! Afraid of moonlight?" sneered a voice. "Off with the winding, man, make haste!"

Many hands tore at the winding sheet. The gleaming cerements fell away, and there appeared a thing of horror—not a body fresh in its youthful beauty, but a skeleton shining as with the phosphorescent light of decay.

There was a scream, an oath, and the Resurrection Men scattered.

"After them!" I cried.

"Be easy, sir," said tall Welch. "My men are ready for them. Come along."

Outside the lych-gate there was a confused scuffle, oaths, the sound of blows. As we passed through, we were surrounded by dark forms of captors and captured.

"You mistake me, good fellows," cried a resonant voice, "I am no body-snatcher, but Lady Julia's friend, Dr. Hardiman, come hither in her interest."

"The surgeon! A friend!" exclaimed the Bow Street man who held him pinioned. "A likely story!"

"See," said the surgeon with a smile, "my hands are clean."

In that darkness it was hardly to be seen whether they were or no; but Dr. Johnson assented at once: "They are so. Unhand him, good fellow."

"And me," exclaimed another captive whose voice I knew. The starlight fell on the lugubrious face of Mr. Blackstock the undertaker.

"Mr. Welch!" he cried. "Bid these boobies re-lease me, for I come on the same errand as you and the surgeon, to see to my dead-watch and baffle the Sack-'em-up Men, and I desire you'll release me at once."

"Stay," said Dr. Johnson, "look at his hands."

"They are clean!" cried Mr. Blackstock.

They may have been clean of graveyard mold, but as tall Welch turned up the palms, they glowed weirdly in the dark.

" 'Tis enough," said Dr. Johnson with satisfaction. "You are caught, sir, if not red-handed, yet with traces on your palms put there by Harlequin's chymically glowing shroud. You are detected, sir; you have gone about to rob your own grave!"

Other glowing palms told the same tale and soon the whole squad of Sack-'em-up Men stood detected. Among them, not at all to my surprise, grinned the sexton. Of course it was he who had disconnected the spring-gun.

"Bravo, Dr. Johnson!" cried a soft voice, as a black-cloaked figure emerged from the church porch. "Your strategem has succeeded!"

Putting back the mourning hood, Lady Julia stood

revealed, smiling and sparkling in the faint light that began to grey the East.

"Shall I have no credit?" A second form stood forth. I stared in disbelief—the fine eyes, the fair face—there stood young Patrick Fitzpatrick, whom I thought I had seen laid in the grave!

"I'm not so easy killed," the boy grinned at my astonishment, "more especially when I find a skilled surgeon to nurse my wound—"

"A meer scratch," murmured Dr. Hardiman. "And the heart's in the right place too."

"To nurse me like a friend," said the youth with emotion, "nay, like a father—"

"Which I yet shall be," smiled the surgeon, and the Lady Julia gave him smile for smile.

"So I mended, and 'twas but lying low for some thirty hours by Dr. Johnson's plan. Nay," said the youth with a schoolboy's relish, " 'twas a splendid bam! Building up a dummy inside Harlequin's gear, with my lady mother's wig stand for a head—and so trapping the villain that stole my father's body!"

The undertaker cursed to himself.

"And there—" The young voice hardened. "—there stands the scoundrel that murdered him!"

The body-snatcher he pointed to started back with an oath.

"I recognized him in the throng at the theatre, lying in wait for me, I doubt not. But before I could dollar him, he nicked me and got away; and hence comes all the rest of this comedy of Dr. Johnson's devising."

"Retribution shall be exacted," said Mr. Welch.

"Conduct them to the round-house."

"So, boy," said Dr. Johnson, "our task is done. Thanks to Mr. De Loutherbourg's chymical paint, which I had of Davy Garrick along with Harlequin's gear, Mr. Blackstock's villainy is detected. He will snatch no more by night the bodies he buries by day; and so farewell to the Resurrection Men!"

[The gruesome profession of the Resurrection Men—digging up dead bodies to be sold for anatomical specimens—was a matter of supply and demand. In Dr. Johnson's day, dissection was legal—if you could get a subject to dissect. Surgeon's Hall got the cadavers of certain criminals condemned to hanging and anatomizing, but with many private anatomical schools going full blast, there were never enough of them to go round. Resurrection Men supplied the rest.

Contests between the bereaved and the Sack-'em-up Men were macabre. It is told in my husband's family how his grandfather and great-uncles in Glasgow, armed, stood guard over their mother's grave by night until they were sure the body had mouldered. Guards, spring-guns, patent-lock iron coffins, "mort-safes" of iron bars, nothing was certain. My story deals with such a contest.

Grave-robbing was worth the effort. A full-grown fresh cadaver might bring four guineas "smalls" one guinea or more according to size. Unique specimens brought more. One anatomist ordered up the body of a man he had operated on twenty-four years before (to see how the patching held up), and it cost him £ 13/12. To obtain the Irish Giant in 1783, Surgeon John Hunter had to pay the dead-watchers a bribe of £500 and transport the naked cadaver in his own coach.

In time, several ingenious Sack-'em-up Men decided it was easier to murder than to dig—Bishop, Williams and May in London, and the famous firm of Burke and Hare in Edinburgh. The exposure of their activities finally brought reform, which put the Resurrection Men out of business. But that is another story.

For more about the Resurrection Men, see James Moore Ball, *The Sack-'em-Up Men* (Edinburgh and London: Oliver and Boyd, 1928).]

MILADY BIGAMY

"I have often thought," remarked Dr. Sam:
Johnson, one Spring morning in the year 1778, "that
if I kept a seraglio—"

He had often thought!—Dr. Sam: Johnson, moral
philosopher, defender of right and justice, *detector* of
crime and chicane, had often thought of keeping a
seraglio! I looked at his square bulk, clad in his
old-fashioned full-skirted coat of plain mulberry
broadcloth, his strong rugged countenance with his
little brown scratch-wig clapped on askew above it,
and suppressed a smile.

"I say, sir, if I kept a seraglio, the houris should be
clad in cotton and linen, and not at all in wool and
silk, for the animal fibres are nasty, but the vegeta-
ble fibres are cleanly."

"Why, sir," I replied seriously, "I too have long
meditated on keeping a seraglio, and wondered
whether it may not be lawful to a man to have
plurality of wives, say one for comfort and another
for shew."

"What, sir, you talk like a heathen Turk!"

growled the great Cham, rounding on me. "If this cozy arrangement be permitted a man, what is to hinder the ladies from a like indulgence?—one husband, say, for support, and 'tother for sport? 'Twill be a wise father then that knows his own heir. You are a lawyer, sir, you know the problems of filiation. Would you multiply them? No, sir: bigamy is a crime, and there's an end on't!"

At this I hastily turned the topick, and of bigamy we spoke no more. Little did we then guess that a question of bigamy was soon to engage my friend's attention, in the affair of the Duchess of Kingsford—if Duchess in truth she was.

I had first beheld this lady some seven years before, when she was Miss Bellona Chamleigh, the notorious Maid of Honour. At Mrs. Cornelys's Venetian ridotto she flashed upon my sight, and took my breath away.

Rumour had not exaggerated her flawless beauty. She had a complection like strawberries and cream, a swelling rosy lip, a nose and firmset chin sculptured in marble. Even the small-pox had spared her, for the one mark it had left her touched the edge of her pouting mouth like a tiny dimple. In stature she was low, a pocket Venus, with a bosom of snow tipped with fire. A single beauty-spot shaped like a new moon adorned her perfect navel—

I go too far. Suffice it to say that for costume she wore a girdle of silken fig-leaves, and personated Eve—Eve after the fall, from the glances she was giving her gallants. One at either rosy elbow, they pressed her close, and she smiled upon them impartially. I recognised them both.

The tall, thin, swarthy, cadaverous apparition in a dark domino was Philip Piercy, Duke of Kingsford, once the handsomest Peer in the Kingdom, but now honed to an edge by a long life of dissipation. If he was no longer the handsomest, he was still the richest. Rumour had it that he was quite far gone in infatuation, and would lay those riches, with his hand and heart, at Miss Bellona's feet.

Would she accept of them? Only one obstacle intervened. That obstacle stood at her other elbow: Captain Aurelius Hart, of H.M.S. *Dangerous*, a third-rate of fifty guns, which now lay fitting at Portsmouth, leaving the gallant Captain free to press his suit.

In person, the Captain was the lady's match, not tall, but broad of shoulder, and justly proportioned in every limb. He had farseeing light blue eyes in a sun-burned face, and his expression was cool, with a look of incipient mirth. The patches of Harlequin set off his muscular masculinity.

With his name too Dame Rumour had been busy. He had won the lady's heart, it was averred; but he was not likely to win her hand, being an impecunious younger son, tho' of an Earl.

So she passed on in her nakedness, giving no sign of which lover—if either—should possess her.

A black-avised young fellow garbed like the Devil watched them go. He scowled upon them with a look so lowering I looked again, and recognised him

for Mr. Eadwin Maynton, Kingsford's nephew,
heir-presumptive to his pelf (tho' not his Dukedom),
being the son of the Duke's sister. If Bellona married
his uncle, it would cost Mr. Eadwin dear.

The audacity of the Maid of Honour at the masquerade had been too blatant. She was forthwith
banished from the Court. Unrepentant, she had rusticated herself. Accompanied only by her confidential woman, one Ann Crannock, she slipped off to
her Aunt Hammer's country houe at Linton, near
Portsmouth.

Near Portsmouth! Where lay the Captain's ship!
No more was needed to inflate the tale.

"The Captain calls daily to press his suit."

"The Captain has taken her into keeping."

"There you are out, the Captain has wedded her
secretly."

"You are all misled. The *Dangerous* has gone to
sea—the Captain has deserted her."

"And serve her right, the hussy!"

The hussy Maid of Honour was not one to be
rusticated for long. Soon she was under their noses
again, on the arm of the still infatuated Duke of
Kingsford. Mr. Eadwin Maynton moved Heaven
and earth to forestall a marriage, but only succeeded
in mortally offending his wealthy uncle. Within a
year of that scandalous masquerade, Miss Bellona
Chamleigh was Duchess of Kingsford.

Appearing at Court on the occasion, she flaunted
herself in white sattin encrusted with Brussels point

and embroidered with a Duke's ransom in pearls. She would give the world something to talk about!

They talked with a will. They talked of Captain Hart, jilted on the Jamaica station. They talked of Mr. Eadwin Maynton sulking at home. They were still talking several years later when the old Duke suddenly died—of his Duchess's obstreperous behaviour, said some with a frown, of her amorous charms, said others with a snigger.

It was at this juncture that one morning in the year '78 a crested coach drew rein in Bolt Court and a lady descended. From an upper window I looked down on her modish tall powdered head and her fur-belowed polonaise of royal purple brocade.

I turned from the window with a smile. "What, sir, you have an assignation with a fine lady? Am I *de trop?*"

"You are never *de trop*, Bozzy. Pray remain, and let us see what this visitation portends."

The Duchess of Kingsford swept in without ceremony.

"Pray forgive me, Dr. Johnson, my errand is to Mr. Boswell. I was directed hither to find him—I *must* have Mr. Boswell!"

"And you *shall* have Mr. Boswell," I cried warmly, "tho' it were for wager of battle!"

"You have hit it, sir! For my honour, perhaps my life, is at stake! You shall defend me, sir, in my need—and Dr. Johnson," she added with a sudden flashing smile, "shall be our counsellor."

"If I am to counsel you, Madam, you must tell me clearly what is the matter."

"Know then, gentlemen, that in the winter last past, my dear husband the Duke of Kingsford died, and left me inconsolable—inconsolable, yet not bare, for in token of our undying devotion, he left me all that was his. In so doing, he cut off his nephew Eadwin with a few guineas, and therein lies the difficulty. For Mr. Eadwin is no friend to me. He has never spared to vilify me for a scheaming adventuress. And now he has hit upon a plan—he thinks—in one motion to disgrace me and deprive me of my inheritance. He goes about to nullify my marriage to the Duke."

"How can this be done, your Grace?"

"He has resurrected the old gossip about Captain Hart, that we were secretly married at Linton long ago. The whole town buzzes with the tale, and the comedians lampoon me on the stage as Milday Bigamy."

"What the comedians play," observed Dr. Johnson drily, "is not evidence. Gossip cannot harm you, your Grace—unless it is true."

"It is false. There was no such marriage. There might have been, it is true (looking pensive) had he not abandoned me, as Aeneas abandoned Dido, and put to sea in the *Dangerous*—leaving me," she added frankly, "to make a better match."

"Then where is the difficulty?"

"False testimony is the difficulty. Aunt Hammer

is dead, and the clergyman is dead. But his widow is alive, and Eadwin has bought her. Worst of all, he has suborned Ann Crannock, my confidential woman that was and she will swear to the wedding."

"Are there marriage lines?"

"Of course not. No marriage, no marriage lines."

"And the Captain? Where is he?"

"At sea. He now commands a first-rate, the *Challenger*, and wins great fame, and much prize money, against the French. I am well assured I am safe in that quarter."

"Then," said I, "this accusation of bigamy is soon answered. But I am not accustomed to appear at the Old Bailey."

"The Old Bailey!" cried she with scorn. "Who speaks of the Old Bailey? Shall a Duchess be tried like a greasy bawd at the Old Bailey? I am the Duchess of Kingsford! I shall be tried by my Peers!"

"If you are Mrs. Aurelius Hart?"

"I am not Mrs. Aurelius Hart! But if I were— Aurelius's brothers are dead in the American war, his father the Earl is no more, and Aurelius is Earl of Westerfell. As Duchess or as Countess, I shall be tried by my Peers!"

Flushed and with flashing eyes, the ci-devant. Maid of Honour looked every inch a Peeress as she uttered these words.

" 'Tis for this I must have Mr. Boswell. From the gallery in the House of Lords I recently heard him plead the cause of the heir of Douglas: in such terms of melting eloquence did he defend the good name of Lady Jane Douglas, I will have no other to defend mine!"

My new role as the Duchess's champion entailed many duties that I had hardly expected. There were of course long consults with herself and her solicitor, a dry, prosy old stick named Pettigree. But I had not counted on attending her strolls in the park, or carrying her bandboxes from the milliner's.

"And to-morrow, Mr. Boswell, you shall squire me to the ridotto."

"The masquerade! Your Grace jests!"

"Far from it, sir. Eadwin Maynton seeks to drive me under ground, but he shall not succeed. No, sir; my heart is set on it, and to the ridotto I will go!"

To the ridotto we went. The Duchess was regal in a domino of Roman purple over a gown of lavender lutestring, and wore a half-mask with a valance of provocative black lace to the chin. I personated a wizard, with my black gown strewn with cabbalistick symbols, and a conical hat to make me tall.

It was a ridotto *al fresco*, in the groves of Vauxhall. In the soft May evening, we listened to the band of musick in the pavilion; we took a syllabub; we walked in the allées to hear the nightingale sing. It was pleasant strolling beneath the young green of the trees by the light of a thousand lamps, watching the masquers pass: a Boadicea in armour, a Hamlet all in black, an Indian Sultana, a muscular Harlequin with a long-nosed Venetian mask, a cowled monk—

"So, Milady Bigamy!" The voice was loud and harsh. "You hide your face, as is fit, but we know you for what you are!"

Passing masquers paused to listen. Pulling the mask from her face, the Duchess whirled on the speaker. A thin swarthy countenance glowered at her under the monk's cowl.

"Eadwin Maynton!" she said quietly. "Why do you pursue me? How have I harmed you? 'Twas your own folly that alienated your kind uncle."

" 'Twas your machinations!" He was perhaps inebriated, and intent on making a scene. More listeners arrived to enjoy it.

"I have irrefutable evidences of your double dealing," he bawled, "and when it comes to the proof, I'll un-duchess you, Milady Bigamy!"

"This fellow is drunk. Come, Mr. Boswell."

The Duchess turned away contemptuously. Mr. Eadwin seized her arm and swung her back. The next minute he was flat on the ground, and a menacing figure in Harlequin's patches stood over him.

"What is your pleasure, Madam?" asked the Harlequin calmly. "Shall he beg pardon?"

"Let him lie," said the Duchess. "He's a liar, let him lie."

"Then be off!"

Maynton made off, muttering.

"And you, ladies and gentlemen, the comedy is over."

Behind the beak-nosed mask, light eyes of ice-blue raked the gapers, and they began to melt away.

"I thank you, my friend. And now, as you say, the comedy is over," smiled the Duchess.

"There is yet a farce to play," said the Harlequin. "*The Fatal Marriage*." He lifted his mask by its snout, and smiled at her. "Who, unless a husband, shall protect his lady wife?"

The Duchess's face stiffened.

"I do not know you."

"What, forgot so soon?" His glance laughed at her. "Such is the fate of the sailor!"

"Do not mock me, Aurelius. You know we are nothing to one another."

"Speak for yourself, Bellona."

"I will speak one word, then: Good-bye."

She reached me her hand, and I led her away. Captain Hart watched us go, his light eyes intent, and a small half-smile upon his lips.

That was the end of Milady Duchess's ridotto. What would come of it?

Nothing good, I feared. My fears were soon doubled. Returning from the river one day in the Duchess's carriage, we found ourselves passing by Mr. Eadwin Moynton's lodging. As we approached, a man issued from the door, an erect figure in nautical blue, whose ruddy countenance wore a satisfied smile. He turned away without a glance in our direction.

"Aurelius calling upon Eadwin!" cried the Duchess, staring after him. "What are they plotting against me?"

To this I had no answer.

Time was running out. The trial was looming close. In Westminster Hall, carpenters were knocking together scaffolding to prepare for the shew. At Kingsford House, Dr. Johnson was quoting Livy, I was polishing my oration, and old Pettigree was digging up learned instances.

"Keep up your heart, your Grace," said the solicitor earnestly in his rusty voice, "for should the worst befall, I have instances to shew that the penalty is no longer death at the stake—"

"At the stake!" gasped the Duchess.

"No, your Grace, certainly not, not death by burning. I shall prove it, but meerly branding on the hand—"

"Branding!" shrieked the Duchess. Her white fingers clutched mine.

"No *alibi*," fretted old Pettigree, "no testimony from Linton on your behalf, Captain Hart in the adverse camp—no, no, your Grace must put your hope in me!"

At such Job's comfort Dr. Johnson could scarce repress a smile.

"Hope rather," he suggested, "in Mr. Boswell, for if these women lie, it must be made manifest in cross-examination. I shall be on hand to note what they say, as I once noted the Parliamentary debates from the gallery; and it will go hard but we shall catch them out in their lies."

Bellona Chamleigh lifted her head in a characteristick wilful gesture.

"I trust in Mr. Boswell, and I am not afraid."

Rising early on the morning of the fateful day, I donned my voluminous black advocate's gown, and a lawyer's powdered wig that I had rented from Tibbs the perruquier for a guinea. I thought that the latter well set off my dark countenance, with its long nose and attentive look. Thus attired, I posted myself betimes outside Westminster Hall to see the procession pass.

At ten o'clock it began. First came the factotums and the functionaries, the yeoman-usher robed, heralds in tabards, sergeants-at-arms with maces in their hands. Then the Peers paced into view, walking two and two, splendid in their crimson velvet mantles and snowy capes of ermine powdered with black tail-tips. Last came the Lord High Steward, his long crimson train borne up behind him, and so they passed into Westminster Hall.

When I entered at last, in my turn as a lowly lawyer, the sight struck me with something like awe. The noble hall, with its soaring roof, was packed to the vault with persons of quality seated upon tier after tier of scaffolding. Silks rustled, laces fluttered, brocades glowed, high powdered foretops rose over all. Around three sides of the level floor gathered the Peers in their splendid robes.

All stood uncovered as the King's Commission was read aloud and the white staff of office was ceremoniously handed up to the Lord High Steward where he sat under a crimson canopy. With a sibilant rustle, the packed hall sat, and the trial began.

"Oyez, oyez, oyez! Bellona, duchess-dowager of Kingsford, come into court!"

She came in a little procession of her own, her ladies of honour, her chaplain, her physician and her apothecary attending; but every staring eye saw her only. Old Pettigree had argued in vain that deep mourning was the only wear; she would have none of it. She walked in proudly in white sattin embroidered with pearls, that very court-dress she had flaunted as old Kingsford's bride: "In token of my innocence," she told old Pettigree.

With a deep triple reverence she took her place on the elevated platform that served for a dock, and stood with lifted head to listen to the indictment.

"Bellona, duchess-dowager of Kingsford, you stand indicted by the name of Bellona, wife of Aurelius Hart, now Earl of Westerfell, for that you, in the eleventh year of our sovereign lord King George the Third, being then married and the wife of the said Aurelius Hart, did marry and take to husband Philip Piercy, Duke of Kingsford, feloniously and with force and arms—"

Though it was the usual legal verbiage to recite that every felony was committed "with force and arms," the picture conjured up of little Bellona, like a highwayman, clapping a pistol to the old Duke's head and marching him to the altar, was too much for the Lords. Laughter swept the benches, and the lady at the bar frankly joined in.

"How say you? Are you guilty of the felony

whereof you stand indicted, or not guilty?"

Silence fell. Bellona sobered, lifted her head, and pronounced in her rich voice: "Not guilty!"

"Culprit, how will you be tried?"

"By God and my Peers."

"Oyez, oyez, oyez! All manner of persons that will give evidence on behalf of our sovereign lord the King, against Bellona, duchess-dowager of Kingsford, let them come forth, and they shall be heard, for now she stands at the bar upon her deliverance."

Thereupon Edward Thurlow, Attorney General, came forth, formidable with his bristling hairy eyebrows and his growling voice like distant thunder.

He began with an eloquent denunciation of the crime of bigamy, its malignant complection, its pernitious example, *et caetera, et caetera.* That duty performed, he drily recited the story of the alleged marriage at Linton as, he said, his witnesses would prove it.

"And now, my Lords, we will proceed to call our witnesses. Call Margery Amys."

Mrs. Amys, the clergyman's widow, was a tall stick of a woman well on in years, wearing rusty bombazine and an old-fashioned lawn cap tied under her nutcracker chin. She put a gnarled hand on the Bible the clerk held out to her.

"Hearken to your oath. The evidence you shall give on behalf of our sovereign lord the King's majesty, against Bellona duchess-dowager of Kingsford, shall be the truth, the whole truth, and nothing but the truth, so help you God."

The old dame mumbled something, and kissed the book. But when the questions began, she spoke up in a rusty screech, and graphically portrayed a clandestine marriage at Linton church in the year '71.

"They came by night, nigh upon midnight, to the church at Linton, and desired of the late Mr. Amys that he should join them two in matrimony."

Q. Which two?

A. Them two, Captain Hart and Miss Bellona Chamleigh.

Q. And did he so unite them?

A. He did so, and I stood by and saw it done.

Q. Who was the bride?

A. Miss Bellona Chamleigh.

Q. Say if you see her now present?

A. (pointing) That's her, her in white.

The Duchess stared her down contemptuously.

As I rose to cross-examine, I sent a glance to the upper tier, where sat Dr. Johnson. He was writing, and frowning as he wrote; but no guidance came my way. Making up with a portentous scowl for what I lacked in matter, I began:

Q. It was dark at midnight?

A. Yes, sir, mirk dark.

Q. Then, Mrs. Amys, how did you see the bride to know her again?

A. Captain Hart lighted a wax taper, and put it in his hat, and by that light they were married, and so I know her again.

Q. (probing) You know a great deal, Madam.

What has Mr. Eadwin Maynton give you to appear
on his behalf?

A. Nothing, sir.

Q. What has he promised you?

A. Nothing neither.

Q. Then why are you here?

A. (piously) I come for the sake of truth and justice, sir.

And on that sanctimonious note, I had to let her
go.

"Call Ann Crannock!"

Ann Crannock approached in a flurry of curtseys,
scattering smiles like sweetmeats. The erstwhile
confidential woman was a plump, round, rosy little
thing, of a certain age, but still pleasing, carefully got
up like a stage milkmaid in snowy kerchief and
pinner. She mounted the platform with a bounce,
and favoured the Attorney General with a beaming
smile.

The Duchess hissed something between her
teeth. It sounded like "Judas!"

The clerk with his Bible hastily stepped between.
Ann Crannock took the oath, smiling broadly, and
Thurlow commenced his interrogation:

Q. You were the prisoner's woman?

A. Yes, sir, and I love her like my own child.

Q. You saw her married to Captain Hart?

A. Yes, sir, the pretty dears, they could not wait
for very lovesickness.

Q. That was at Linton in July of the year 1771?

A. Yes, sir, the third of July, for the Captain sailed

with the Jamaica squadron on the fourth. Ah, the sweet poppets, they were loth to part!

Q. Who married them?

A. Mr. Amys, sir, the vicar of Linton. We walked to the church together, the lady's Aunt Mrs. Hammer, and I myself, and the sweet lovebirds. The clock was going towards midnight, that the servants might not know.

Q. Why must not the servants know?

A. Sir, nobody was to know, lest the Captain's father the Earl cut him off for marrying a lady without any fortune.

Q. Well, and they were married by Mr. Amys. Did he give a certificate of the marriage?

A. Yes, sir, he did, he wrote it out with his own hand, and I signed for a witness. I was happy for my lady from my heart.

Q. You say the vicar gave a certificate. (Thurlow sharply raised his voice as he whipped out a paper.) Is this it?

A. (clasping her hands and beaming with pleasure) O sir, that is it. See, there is my handwriting. Well I mind how the Captain kissed it and put it in his bosom to keep!

" 'Tis false!"

The Duchess was on her feet in a rage. For a breath she stood so in her white sattin and pearls; then she sank down in a swoon. Her attendants instantly raised her and bore her out among them. I saw the little apothecary hopping like a grasshopper on the fringes, flourishing his hartshorn bottle.

The Peers were glad enough of an excuse for a recess, and so was I. I pushed my way to the lobby in search of Dr. Johnson. I was furious. "The jade has lied to us!" I cried as I beheld him. "I'll throw up my brief!"

"You will do well to do so," murmured the Attorney General at my elbow. He still held the fatal marriage lines.

"Pray, Mr. Thurlow, give me a sight of that paper," requested Dr. Johnson.

"Dr. Johnson's wish is my command," said Thurlow with a bow: he had a particular regard for the burly philosopher.

Dr. Johnson held the paper to the light, peering so close with his near-sighted eyes that his lashes almost brushed the surface.

"Aye, sir, look close," smiled Thurlow. " 'Tis authentick, I assure you. I have particular reason to know."

"Then there's no more to be said."

Thurlow took the paper, bowed, and withdrew.

All along I had been conscious of another legal figure hovering near. Now I looked at him directly. He was hunched into a voluminous advocate's gown, and topped by one of Mr. Tibbs's largest wigs; but there was no missing those ice-blue eyes.

"Captain Hart! You here?"

"I had a mind to see the last of my widow," he said sardonically. "I see she is in good hands."

"But to come here! Will you not be recognised, and detained, and put on the stand?"

"What, Peers detain a Peer? No, sir. While the

House sits, I cannot be summoned: and when it rises, all is over. Bellona may be easy; I shan't peach. Adieu."

"Stay, sir—" But he was gone.

After an hour, the Duchess of Kingsford returned to the hall with her head held high, and inquiry resumed. There was not much more harm Mistress Crannock could do. Sye was led once more to repeat: she saw them wedded, the sweet dears, and she signed the marriage lines, and that was the very paper now in Mr. Thurlow's hand.

"You say this is the paper? That is conclusive, I think. (smiling) You may cross-examine, Mr. Boswell."

Ann Crannock smiled at me, and I smiled back, as I began:

Q. You say, Mistress Crannock, that you witnessed this marriage?

A. Yes, sir.

Q. And then and there you signed the marriage lines?

A. Yes, sir.

Q. On July 3, 1771?

A. Yes, sir.

Q. Think well, did you not set your hand to it at some subsequent date?

A. No, sir.

Q. Perhaps to oblige Mr. Eadwin Maynton?

A. No, sir, certainly not. I saw them wedded, and signed forthwith.

Q. Then I put it to you: *How did you on July 3,*

1771, set your hand to a piece of paper that was not made at the manufactory until the year 1774?

Ann Crannock turned red, then pale, opened her mouth, but no sound came. "Can you make that good. Mr. Boswell?" demanded Thurlow.

"Yes, sir, if I may call a witness, tho' out of order."

"Aye, call him—let's hear him—" the answer swept the Peers' benches. Their Lordships cared nothing for order.

"I call Dr. Samuel Johnson."

Dr. Johnson advanced and executed one of his stately obeisances.

"You must know, my Lords and gentlemen," he began, "that I have dealt with paper for half a century, and I have friends among the paper-makers. Paper, my Lords, is made by grinding up rag, and wetting it, and laying it to dry upon a grid of wires. Now he who has a mind to sign his work, twists his mark in wire and lays it in, for every wire leaves its impression, which is called a watermark. With such a mark, in the shape of an S, did my friend Sully the paper-maker sign the papers he made before the year '74.

"But in that year, my Lords, he took his son into partnership, and from thenceforth marked his paper with a double S. I took occasion this afternoon to confirm the date, 1774, from his own mouth. Now, my Lords, if you take this supposed document of 1771 (taking it in his hand) and hold it thus to the light, you may see in it the double S watermark: which, my Lords, proves this so-called conclusive evidence to be a forgery, and Ann Crannock a liar!"

The paper passed from hand to hand, and the Lord began to seethe.

"The Question! The Question!" was the cry. The clamour persisted, and did not cease until perforce the Lord High Steward arose, bared his head, and put the question:

"Is the prisoner guilty of the felony whereof she stands indicted, or not guilty?"

In a breathless hush, the first of the barons rose in his robes, Bellona lifted her chin. The young nobleman put his right hand upon his heart and pronounced clearly:

"Not guilty, upon my honour!"

So said each and every Peer:

"Not guilty, upon my honour!"

My client was acquitted!

At her Grace's desire, I had provided means whereby, at the trial's end, come good fortune or ill, the Duchess might escape the press of the populace. A plain coach waited at a postern door, and thither, her white sattin and pearls muffled in a capuchin, my friend and I hurried her.

Quickly she mounted the step and slipped inside. Suddenly she screamed. Inside the coach a man awaited us. Captain Aurelius Hart in his blue coat lounged there at his ease.

"Nay, sweet wife, my wife no more," he murmured softly, "do not shun me, for now that you are decreed to be another man's widow, I mean to woo you anew. I have prepared a small victory feast at my lodgings, and I hope your friends will do us the honour of partaking of it with us."

"Victory!" breathed Bellona as the coach moved us off. "How could you be so sure of victory?"

"Because," said Dr. Johnson, "he brought it about. Am I not right, sir?"

"Why, sir, as to that—"

"As to that, sir, there is no need to prevaricate. I learned this afternoon from Sully the paper-maker that a seafaring man resembling Captain Hart had been at him last week to learn about papers, and had carried away a sheet of the double S kind. It is clear that it was you, sir, who foisted upon Eadwin Maynton the forgery that, being exposed, defeated him."

All this while the coach was carrying us onward. In the shadowy interior, Captain Hart frankly grinned.

" 'Twas easy, sir. Mr. Eadwin was eager, and quite without scruple, and why should he doubt a paper that came from the hands of the wronged husband? How could he guess that I had carefully contrived it to ruin his cause?"

"It was a bad cause," said Dr. Johnson, "and he is well paid for his lack of scruple."

"But, Captain Hart," I put in, "how could you be sure that we would detect the forgery and proclaim it?"

"To make sure, I muffled up and ventured into the lobby. I was prepared to slip a billet into Mr. Boswell's pocket; but when I saw Dr. Johnson studying the watermark, I knew that I need not interfere further."

We were at the door. Captain Hart lifted down the lady, and with his arm around her guided her up the stair. She yielded mutely, as in a daze.

In the withdrawing room a pleasing cold regale awaited us, but Dr. Johnson was in no hurry to go to table. There was still something on his mind.

"Then, sir, before we break bread, satisfy me of one more thing. How came Ann Crannock to say the handwriting was hers?"

"Because, sir," said Captain Hart with a self-satisfied look, "it was so like her own. I find I have a pretty turn for forgery."

"That I can believe, sir. But where did you find an exemplar to fashion your forgery after?"

"Why, sir, I—" The Captain darted a glance from face to face. "You are keen, sir. There could only be one document to forge after—and here it is (producing a folded paper from his pocket). Behold the true charter of my happiness!"

I regarded it thunderstruck. A little faded as to ink, a little frayed at the edges, there lay before us a marriage certificate in due form, between Miss Bellona Chamleigh, spinster, and Captain Aurelius Hart, bachelor, drawn up in the Reverend Mr. Amys's wavering hand, and attested by Sophie Hammer and Ann Crannock, July 3, 1771!

"So, Madam," growled Dr. Johnson, "you were guilty after all!"

"Oh, no, sir! 'Twas no marriage, for the Captain was recalled to his ship, and sailed for the Jamaica station, without—without—"

"Without making you in deed and in truth my own," smiled Captain Hart.

At this specimen of legal reasoning, Dr. Johnson shook his head in bafflement, the bigamous Duchess looked as innocent as possible, and Captain Hart laughed aloud.

" 'Twas an unfortunate omission," he said, "whence flow all our uneasinesses, and I shall rectify it this night, my Countess consenting. What do you say, my dear?"

For the first time the Duchess looked directly at him. In spite of herself she blushed, and the tiny pox mark beside her lips deepened in a smile.

"Why, Aurelius, since you have saved me from branding or worse, what can I say but yes?"

"Then at last," cried the Captain, embracing her, "you shall be well and truly bedded, and so farewell to the Duchess of Kingsford!"

It seemed the moment to withdraw. As we descended, we heard them laughing together.

"Never look so put about, Bozzy," murmured Dr. Johnson on the stair. "You have won your case; justice, tho'irregularly, is done; the malignancy of Eadwin Maynton has been defeated; and as to the two above—they deserve each other."

✥

[The Dutchess of Kingston was tried for bigamy by her Peers in April, 1778. The trial was just such a Roman holiday as I have depicted, and Boswell was there to see it. What impressed him most was the towering coiffures of the ladies. The Peers did not impress him. He had in fact argued the Douglas cause before them not long before.

Unsuitably for fiction, the Duchess of Kingston was fifty-five years old, she weighed fourteen stone, and, wearing the proper mourning garb, she looked to the spectators like "a bale of bombazine." Furthermore, she was found guilty, escaping the branding-iron by "pleading her clergy," that is, by maintaining she could read and write, which by an antiquated legalism got her off. Her full story is told in Elizabeth Mavor's *The Virgin Mistress* (New York, Doubleday & Company, Inc., 1964).

Johnson's seraglio, which opens my story, came under discussion during the Scotch visit, and Boswell's japes on the subject got him a sharp reprimand. Boswell always had a secret yen to keep a harem himself.]

ACKNOWLEDGMENTS

For help and encouragement I have many people
to thank:

My regretted friends and mentors Ellery Queen
(Frederic Dannay) and Lewis M. Knapp.

Eleanor Sullivan, editor and friend

Librarians Kee DeBoer, George Fagan, Ellsworth
Mason

Generous helpers Frank Krutzke, Ellen and Vin-
cent O'Brien, Dorothy and Paul Thompson.

British Friends Stella and Geoffrey Ward, Char-
lotte and Denis Plimmer, Margot Bronner.

And always my husband, George S. McCue, upon
whose wide learning, critical judgment and penetrating insights I depend.

Lillian de la Torre

ABOUT THE AUTHOR

Lillian de la Torre was born in New York on March 15, 1902, and christened Lillian de la Torre Bueno (subsequently shortening the name to provide her pseudonym). She was brought up in a house full of books, including a rich collection of early detective stories, which marked her for life. In graduate school her field of special interest was the Age of Johnson, soon to provide both the inspiration and the materials for her continuing short story series about Dr. Sam: Johnson, detector.

As the wife of George S. McCue of Colorado College (now retired), Miss de la Torre has spent almost fifty productive years in Colorado Springs, Colorado.

Half of her twelve published books are in her chosen field of historical mystery and crime, including *Elizabeth Is Missing*, *The Heir of Douglas*, *The Truth about Belle Gunness*, and a play, *Goodbye, Miss Lizzie Borden*. Two biographies for teens, an anthology, and two cook books (co-authored), and a collection of verse, with numerous articles both "learned" and otherwise, complete the list.

Her hobbies are amateur theatre as actress and playwright, choral singing, travel for pleasure as well as research, and cooking, a daily adventure.

Still active, Miss de la Torre is now working on the mystery of the "Kidnapped Earl," and her "Dr. Sam: Johnson, detector" short stories continue to appear now and then in *Ellery Queen's Mystery Magazine*.